Kai could hear the cheers and hoots before the ride even ended. There'd definitely been luck involved. Somehow he'd found himself on a wave that didn't want to quit. But he'd also taken advantage of what it had to offer.

When he paddled back out, Kai wasn't surprised to see the glum expression on Lucas's face. The guy knew he'd been completely outsurfed. What did surprise Kai was when Lucas nodded and grudgingly said, "Nice ride."

Kai paddled up over the next wave. There was Spazzy, sitting on his board, shoulders hunched, looking even more bummed than Lucas.

Only then did Kai realize what he'd done.

D1569998

Look for the final book in the
Impact Zone series:

Close Out

Coming soon from Simon Pulse

And get hooked on some of Todd Strasser's
other Simon & Schuster books . . .

Can't Get There from Here
Give a Boy a Gun
How I Created My Perfect Prom Date
Here Comes Heavenly
Buzzard's Feast: Against the Odds

TWINSBURG LIBRARY
TWINSBURG OHIO

IMPACT ZONE

CUT BACK

TODD STRASSER

i 06898 10 302   Y/A
                   S
                   #2

Simon Pulse
New York   London   Toronto   Sydney

If you purchased this book without a cover, you should be aware that this book is stolen property. It was reported as "unsold and destroyed" to the publisher, and neither the author nor the publisher has received any payment for this "stripped book."

This book is a work of fiction. Any references to historical events, real people, or real locales are used fictitiously. Other names, characters, places, and incidents are the product of the author's imagination, and any resemblance to actual events or locales or persons, living or dead, is entirely coincidental.

First Simon Pulse edition June 2004

Text copyright © 2004 by Todd Strasser

SIMON PULSE
An imprint of Simon & Schuster
Children's Publishing Division
1230 Avenue of the Americas
New York, NY 10020

All rights reserved, including the right of reproduction in whole or in part in any form.

SIMON PULSE and colophon are registered trademarks of Simon & Schuster, Inc.

Designed by Ann Sullivan
The text of this book was set in Bembo.

Printed in the United States of America
10 9 8 7 6 5 4 3 2 1

Library of Congress Control Number 2003115438

ISBN 0-689-87030-2

In memory of Jill Tuck, as fine a mother, surfer's wife, and all-around wonderful person as most of us will ever have the privilege to know

This book is dedicated to Geoff and Lia, my favorite surfing companions.

One

Kai Herter thought he was seeing things.

It was a little after 7 A.M. and he was walking down the sidewalk toward Sun Haven beach with his new thruster under his arm. The sun was already up, the breeze was off-shore, and he was eager to get his first look at the waves. Ahead of him in the parking lot next to the boardwalk, his friends Bean and Booger were getting out of what looked exactly like a long black hearse.

A hearse?

"Hey, dude." Bean gave Kai a wave.

Kai gestured at the black car, which had long narrow windows along the sides covered by gray curtains. "What's the story?"

"These are the great wheels he's been talking about," Booger said, sounding kind of disgusted. "Creeps you out, doesn't it?"

"I got a deal I couldn't refuse," Bean said.

"How's that?" Kai asked.

"His father's the town undertaker," Booger said. "Dr. Death, remember?"

Kai recalled that a month ago, shortly after he'd met these guys, Booger had said something about Bean going to mortuary college in the fall.

"It's a perfect vehicle for transporting surfboards," Bean said.

"Except for those dumb frilly curtains along the back windows," said Booger.

"Don't want anyone to see inside," Bean said. "Creates an air of mystery. You never know, maybe there's a stiff back there." He pulled open the back door and slid out a couple of long, gray two-by-fours.

"Building a new surfboard?" Kai joked.

"Fourth of July," Bean said.

Kai looked in the back of the hearse. There were three surfboard racks along the right side. In the highest rack was Bean's long board, but in the racks beneath it and piled on the left side was a bunch of scrap wood.

"For a cookout?" Kai asked.

"Bonfire." Booger reached into the back and pulled out some large scraps of plywood. "We all build 'em along the beach."

"I can carry something," Kai offered.

Bean handed him a broken wooden shelf. With the wood under his left arm and his thruster under his right, Kai joined his friends as they crossed the boardwalk and walked onto the beach. Out at the break called Screamers, Lucas Frank and his crew were bobbing on their surfboards, dividing their time between scanning the horizon for the next set of good waves, and keeping an eye on Kai and his friends.

"You going back out there?" Bean asked Kai as they walked.

"Why not?" Kai said.

"I'll tell you why not," Booger said. "Because that's one mad beautiful stick Teddy gave you. You take it out there and Sam is liable to run you down again."

Slammin' Sam was the "muscle" in Lucas's crew. A classic case of too much brawn and not enough brain. Five days ago Kai had surfed against him for the right to open the lineup at Screamers to anyone who wanted to surf there.

"Sam and I had a talk about that," Kai said.

3

"I basically told him that if he ever dings one of my boards again, he's gonna be wearing my leash as a permanent choker."

They dropped the wood in a pile directly opposite the break called Sewers. Booger looked down the beach. "Lucas and his guys haven't even started building their bonfire yet."

"They always get help," Bean said.

Kai kneeled down and started to wax the pearl white custom board Teddy had "given" him for the heat against Sam. It wasn't a gift really. It had been given to him with the understanding that he would pay her back for it. Kai hadn't used the board since the heat with Sam. The morning after the heat, the wind had turned southwest, kicking up whitecaps and closing out Screamers as waves bashed into the jetty. For the past four days the local breaks had been unsurfable. Kai had spent the mornings doing ding repairs at Teddy's and the days and nights working at T-licious, his father's bogus T-shirt shop.

This morning the winds were finally offshore again. The waves were shifty and short. A lot of sections and closeouts, but now and then one peeled nicely for a few dozen yards—long enough to have some fun.

A loud hoot came from the direction of Screamers. Kai, Bean, and Booger looked up in time to see Lucas tearing up a left.

"He's rippin' harder this year than he was last year," Bean said.

"He should be," Booger said, "considering his dad took him to Hawaii for two weeks over Christmas, and a week down in Costa over Easter."

"Business at the surf shop must be good," Kai said. Lucas's father, Buzzy Frank, owned Sun Haven Surf, the big shop in town.

"Not just the surf shop, dude," Bean said. "Buzzy owns a lot of real estate around here."

That made sense. No wonder Buzzy was so interested in getting rid of Curtis and the rundown Driftwood Motel. Curtis was a crusty old guy whose motel catered to low-budget surfers. Once that "eyesore" was gone, Buzzy's other properties were bound to increase in value.

"Hey, guys." Shauna came down the beach with Kai's long board under her arm. She was just learning to surf, and now that Kai had the thruster, he'd lent her old #43. Curtis had given him that board, and his wet suit, when Kai first got to Sun Haven.

"Hey, Shauna," Kai and Bean both answered.

"There goes Everett," Booger said, directing their attention back to Screamers. Everett, a thin, agile black kid with dreadlocks had just caught a wave. Instead of the attacking, slash-and-bash, cram-in-as-many-moves-as-possible style of Lucas, Everett streaked along the face, building up speed until the wave closed out in front of him. He compressed and launched himself high into the air. Kicking his board away, he tucked his arms around his knees, did a flip over the back of the wave, and disappeared. The leash stretched tight and the board rocketed down behind him.

"Don't try this at home, children," Bean quipped.

"I hope the board didn't hit him." Shauna sounded worried.

Kai felt a grin grow on his face.

"What's funny?" Booger asked.

"Not really funny," Kai said. "Just cool to see someone do something like that, you know? It's not gonna score any points in a heat, but it sure looks like fun."

"Come on, Boogs, let's get the rest of the wood out of the car." Bean headed back up the beach. Kai kneeled down and finished waxing.

"You going to Screamers?" Shauna asked.

"Absolutely," Kai answered.

"Be careful," she said.

Kai winked at her, then picked up the thruster, took off down the beach, and launched himself into the water.

Two

There were two ways to get out to Screamers. The easy way was to paddle into the natural channel along the jetty. The harder way was to go with the backwash between Screamers and Sewers. That was the way Kai chose, since it would allow him to catch up to Everett.

Kai paddled out. For the past week the ocean had been gradually getting warmer, but not in a steady way. Some mornings the water temperature was in the higher end of the sixties and Kai felt like he could have gone out there in a shorty wet suit or even a neoprene rash guard. The next morning it would be back in the low sixties and he was glad to have the full wet suit.

He caught up to Everett about halfway back out.

"Yo," Kai said. "Looked like you enjoyed yourself on that last ride."

Everett turned with a look of surprise on his face. "You saw that?"

"Hard to miss," Kai said.

"Yeah, well, sometimes you catch it just right." Everett grinned, obviously pleased with himself. Suddenly his expression changed and the grin disappeared. "Uh, well, see ya."

He started to paddle away. Kai knew what had just happened. For a moment, Everett had forgotten whose crew he was with, and they were just two guys who loved the water and surfing and messing around in the waves. Then Everett must have remembered that Kai was "the enemy." It was so incredibly stupid.

Kai got outside Screamers and found Lucas, Sam, Runt, and some others waiting for him. The vibe was heavy. There was one new guy in particular—medium-size, but with a strong build, short black hair, serious tattoos on his arms and back, an earring, and a bar through his eyebrow. While Slammin' Sam was a straight-ahead brawler with the brains of a tree stump, there was something more ominous about this new guy.

"What are you doing here?" Sam asked Kai.

"Surfing," Kai answered. "How about you?"

"I thought the deal was you could only surf here if you won the heat," said Sam.

"Some people think I did win," Kai said.

Sam smirked. "That's an awful nice-looking stick."

"I told you what's gonna happen if you touch it," Kai warned him.

A new set was approaching. Kai could see Lucas's crew eyeing the waves, then looking at Lucas, as if they didn't know what to do.

"We all just gonna sit here giving each other the stink eye while these nice waves go past?" Kai asked.

"Hey, feel free to take one," Sam said.

"After you," Kai said.

"Take a wave, Sam," Lucas said. "This is stupid."

Sam took off. Kai waited for the others to catch waves, just to show them again that he believed waves could be shared. Finally a medium-size A-frame popped up. Kai turned his board around and paddled into it. The new thruster had an uncanny combination of maneuverability and stability, and like Everett, Kai went for pure speed, wriggling along the face of the wave, then suddenly cutting back up into the corner, then heading back down and picking up speed again. The ride felt like it could be a long one, and Kai played along the feathering lip until the wave closed out into an eruption of white foam.

About fifteen feet from the shore he hopped off the board, tucked it under his arm and walked the rest of the way in. After four days of no surf, it always amazed him how jazzed he could feel after that first good ride. He stopped on the beach and looked out toward Sewers. By now Bean and Booger had finished carrying the firewood down to the beach and had changed into their wet suits and headed out into the water. Bean and Shauna were sitting on their long boards, waiting for a wave. Booger, being a spongehead, was farther inside.

A smallish wave was coming and Bean let Shauna take it. Rather than grab the wave himself, Bean had clearly looked it over and decided it was better for a beginner. Shauna got prone and started to paddle. Like a lot of new surfers, she suddenly paused to adjust her position on the board, then started paddling again, completely neglecting to keep an eye on the wave approaching behind her. The wave crested early and started to fold over her. Kai winced as he watched Shauna grab the rails of the board and pearl into the trough, disappearing into a cloudburst of white. A moment later the board shot straight up out of the boil like a rocket, turned sideways in the air, and fell back down. Kai realized he was holding his breath while he waited to make sure it hadn't smashed her on the head or cut her with its skeg.

Shauna's head popped up in the white soup. She grabbed the leash, pulled the board toward her, got on, and started to paddle back out. The girl had spunk.

Kai turned and walked along the beach toward the jetty. After nearly a month of surfing around Sun Haven, he was beginning to understand the tides and currents. A southwest swell made Screamers unsurfable, but opened up a few lesser breaks up and down the shoreline. A swell directly out of the south produced some sectiony waves at Screamers, but a southeast swell could turn the spot into a point break with wave after wave peeling away into perfection.

Kai got to the jetty, threw himself and the board into the water, and started to paddle. In almost no time he was outside Screamers with Lucas and his crew. Runt seriously vibed him and Kai just smiled back. The red-haired kid scowled and looked away as if he didn't know how to react. Runt would have made a good Nazi.

Kai was waiting for the next good wave when Lucas paddled out near him.

"You hear about the contest over in Fairport?" he asked.

Kai shook his head.

"It's in a couple of weeks," Lucas said. "Me and my friends'll all be there. I figure a surfer as good as you will be there too."

Kai just gazed at the waves and said nothing.

"Or maybe it's too small for you," Lucas said. "I mean, it's just a rinky-dink local contest. Maybe you only surf the WCT."

The WCT was the World Championship Tour, surfed by the best surfers in the world. Kai knew Lucas was just trying to rile him. "That's the kind of crap I expect from Sam, not from you. Cut to the chase, Lucas."

"Some people think all this free surfing, soul surfing garbage is a pose," Lucas said. "Just an easy excuse for not competing."

"What's so important about competing?" Kai asked.

"If it wasn't important, why would there be all these competitions?" Lucas asked. "Why does every kid dream of being the next Pipe Master?"

"Maybe every kid *you* know," Kai replied. "Maybe the only reason competitions exist is because without them, sunglass and shoe companies wouldn't know who to feature in their ads."

"It's funny about some guys," Lucas said. "They surf pretty good when there's no pressure, but as soon as it counts, they fold like a limp rag."

"Is that what it's all about?" Kai shot back. "You think when Duke Kahanamoku traveled around the world demonstrating surfing, he told everybody that the whole idea was performing under pressure?"

"Maybe not then," Lucas said. "But it is now. Because otherwise, all you'll ever be is the best surfer no one ever heard of."

"What's wrong with that?" Kai asked.

"What's wrong with surfing because it's something you love, and it doesn't matter who knows?"

"Go ask your friend Curtis," Lucas said.

"Because he used to run the local contests around here?" Kai guessed.

"Is that what he told you?" Lucas said. "He didn't tell you about surfing all over the world?"

"Yeah, he mentioned that he'd been around," Kai said.

"Ever stop and wonder how he did it?" Lucas asked. "I mean, travel around the world year after year, surfing the best breaks on the planet?"

A good wave was coming and Kai decided to paddle over and catch it.

The last thing he heard Lucas say was, "You should ask him."

Three

Kai surfed until nine thirty. His dad's T-shirt shop, T-licious, opened each morning at 10 A.M., and Kai was expected to be there. But that wasn't the only reason he was stopping. As the month of June wound down, schools all over the northeast had closed, and the beaches at Sun Haven had begun to get more and more crowded. Even on "cold-water" days like this, by 10 A.M. there were enough swimmers in the water to make the surfing a little hairy. A lot of swimmers didn't seem to understand that playing in a wave ten feet ahead of a rapidly approaching surfboard could have seriously unpleasant results.

Kai rode his last wave all the way in. By

now the day was starting to heat up. Beach umbrellas were beginning to blossom like flowers. Towels and blankets were being spread as families and groups of teens settled in for a day of sun and fun. Kai pulled the zipper down the back of his wet suit and peeled the black rubber off his arms and shoulders and down to his waist. Then he wrapped the leash of his board around the tail.

Out of the corner of his eye he noticed someone coming along the beach toward him. It was a guy, probably about Kai's age, trotting in a weird, herky-jerky manner. His hands moved in strange, twitchy motions, and his head rolled and snapped. To Kai it almost seemed like there were two people inside the guy's body, both fighting for control over what he did. The whole effect was so bizarre that Kai actually stared.

The guy stopped half a dozen feet away, as if he knew better than to get too close.

He started to hop up and down, licking his lips with his tongue. He may have been trying to say something, but it was hard to tell. The only sound he made was "Scree . . . scree . . . scree," like he was a crow or something. The whole thing was so whacked that Kai actually looked around to see if someone was playing a joke on him.

But no one he knew was watching. Over at Screamers, Lucas and his crew were busy catching waves, while a hundred yards to the right, Bean, Booger, and Shauna were doing the same thing at Sewers. Meanwhile this guy seemed to be working himself into a frenzy, as if he was trying to do something, but the harder he tried, the more he jerked and grimaced and hopped and squeaked.

Finally a massive shudder shook through him, as if his whole body had gone on overload and shut down. His shoulders sagged and his jerky legs and arms went limp. He shook his head and turned away. Strangely, while he still jerked and flinched slightly, it was nothing like before.

Now something else caught Kai's attention. A dark green dump truck with TOWN OF SUN HAVEN written on the side was weaving through the blankets and umbrellas along the beach. The back was piled high with scrap wood. The truck stopped directly inshore from Screamers, and Dave McAllister, the stocky red-haired chairman of the Sun Haven Surf boardroom, jumped out along with two guys wearing light green Town of Sun Haven coveralls. Big Dave pointed at a spot on the sand and the two town employees climbed into the back of the truck and started tossing out the scrap wood.

Kai watched with interest. He had to assume that delivering scrap wood for Fourth of July bonfires wasn't part of a typical town employee's job description. Dave McAllister worked for Buzzy Frank, Lucas's father, not for the town. Yet, there he was giving orders to the two guys off-loading the wood. If Buzzy Frank didn't outright own the town of Sun Haven, he sure came close.

Kai started up the beach. The strange guy had stopped about a hundred feet away and was watching him. He and Kai exchanged another look. It seemed as if there was something the guy urgently wanted to communicate, but was unable to. Kai felt bad, but it wasn't his problem.

Four

Kai had just let himself in through the back door of the T-shirt shop when Pat came into the back room and handed him a credit card. "Run off a charge for two hundred and sixty plus tax, and ten blanks of this," the Alien Frog Beast from planet Dimwit ordered, adjusting his thick, square-framed glasses. Then Kai's father disappeared through the back door that led to the parking lot outside.

Kai looked down at the silver card. A Fuji Bank Visa. Clearly from Japan. This was one of Pat's favorite scams. Anytime he got his hands on a foreign credit card, he'd run off blanks and then overnight them to certain "business associates" he knew in Nevada who used forged signatures to get cash advances. By the time the tourists from Japan got home and found out they'd been scammed out of thousands of dollars, they'd be halfway around the world and unable to do anything about it.

Kai laid the credit card on the desk where the pile of unopened mail was growing larger every day. Not only did Pat never throw out garbage—electing instead to let food wrappers, papers, and junk fall to the floor—but he also never opened mail. After all, the only mail that came to the store was junk and bills, and since Pat never paid bills, he saw no reason to look at them.

One letter, however, caught Kai's eye. It was addressed to a Mr. Pat Garrison and had a cancelled stamp instead of the usual red postal machine mark that was the sign of junk mail and bills. Kai slid it out from the pile of unopened envelopes and took a closer look. The return address was EBF Realty, 467 Seaside Highway, Sun Haven, and it looked both personal and official. Kai tore it open.

DEAR MR. GARRISON,

IT HAS COME TO OUR ATTENTION THAT YOU AND YOUR SONS ARE LIVING FULL TIME IN THE STOREFRONT PREMISES WE HAVE LEASED TO YOU AT 3 EAST STREET,

SUN HAVEN. PLEASE NOTE THAT SUCH INHABITATION IS A VIOLATION OF YOUR LEASE AGREEMENT. WE REQUEST THAT YOU FIND APPROPRIATE LIVING ARRANGEMENTS IMMEDIATELY. FAILURE TO DO SO WILL CONSTITUTE A VIOLATION OF YOUR LEASE AGREEMENT AND WILL RESULT IN EVICTION AND FORFEITURE OF YOUR SECURITY DEPOSIT.

SINCERELY,

EBF REALTY

The back door opened and Pat came back in. "Got those blanks?"

"No," said Kai.

"What the hell?"

"I'm not helping you rip people off," Kai said.

"Damn you." His father scooped the credit card off the table and started running blanks from it in the credit card machine.

"You might be interested in this." Kai held up the envelope.

"What is it?" Pat asked.

"Letter from your landlord saying they know we're living here and if we don't move out they're going to evict us and keep the security deposit."

"Screw 'em," Pat said.

"This letter was dated almost two weeks ago," Kai said. "I wouldn't be surprised if you hear from them again soon."

His father shrugged as if he didn't care. He finished running the credit card blanks, and headed out to the front. Kai followed him, curious to see who was getting scammed this time.

Out in the store a Japanese man, his wife, and two children were all having custom T-shirts made that said, "We've been to Sun Haven" on the front and had one of the nicer and more overpriced, colorful transfers of a sunset on the back.

"Here you go, Mr. Asoki." Pat handed the credit card back to the man. "I've taken care of the credit verification. Before I forget, do you want color guard on these shirts?"

Kai glanced over Pat's shoulder at a pad on the counter on which his father had written "$260." Kai quickly did the math. Two hundred and sixty dollars for four T-shirts came to sixty-five dollars a shirt. That was close to a new record. The Alien Frog Beast must have been in heaven.

"What is color guard?" Mr. Asoki asked.

Pat pointed at the colorful sunsets on the backs of the shirts. "So when you wash these clothes, the colors don't run."

"Run?" Mr. Asoki scowled.

"Come off." Pat gestured. "So the colors don't get on the other clothes in the wash."

"Ah." Mr. Asoki nodded and spoke to his wife in Japanese, then turned back to Pat. "How much is color guard?"

"Usually ten dollars per shirt, but since you're buying four, I'll do them all for thirty dollars. Of course, it'll have to be cash since I already put the charge through on your credit card."

"Very good," said Mr. Asoki.

Kai's calculation had just increased the total charge to two hundred and ninety dollars. That plus the tax, which Pat charged but never filed with the state, put the total bill over three hundred dollars. Slightly more than seventy-five dollars a shirt. Definitely a new record.

Pat handed the T-shirts to Kai. "Color guard."

Kai hesitated. There was no such thing as color guard. It was just another scam. The colors in the heat transfers never ran. All he was supposed to do was take the shirts in the back, wait a suitable amount of time, then bring them out front again. Usually Kai refused to participate in Pat's scams, but he knew today it wouldn't matter. If he didn't do it, Pat would have Sean do it, or Pat would do it himself. Either way, Mr. Asoki was going to get soaked.

Kai took the shirts into the back room and dropped them on the desk. Once again he gazed down at the pile of unopened bills, the blank credit card receipts, and the landlord's letter lying on the desk. Bills that would never be paid. Receipts that would be used fraudulently. A letter that would probably be ignored. It all meant the same thing. The clock had officially begun to tick. How much time was left before the bill collectors started calling? Before the phone and electric were turned off? Before an investigator from the credit card company knocked on the door? Before the landlord changed the locks?

Kai's time in Sun Haven was starting to run out. Sooner or later it would mean another 3 A.M. escape. Another two- or three-day drive. Another resort town with unsuspecting victims to scam. There was only one thing Kai could be reasonably certain of. The next place wouldn't have a beach, waves, or surfing.

Five

At dinnertime Pat gave Kai five dollars and the usual warning to be back at the T-shirt shop in fifteen minutes or else. The "else" part made Kai laugh. There was nothing Pat could do if he was late. Recently Kai had gotten into the habit of taking as long as he wanted for dinner.

Tonight he was feeling hungry. The five bucks wasn't even enough for two slices of pizza and a Coke. The balance came from whatever he had in his pocket, but after he'd eaten the two slices, Kai was still hungry. The answer was a stop at the shop where Shauna worked, a thin sliver of a place simply called Ice Cream.

As usual on a warm summer night in Sun Haven, there was a line out the door and onto the sidewalk. Through the window Kai could see Shauna and two boys behind the counter. All three were wearing bright green T-shirts that said, "I Scream for Ice Cream." Kai got in line behind three young women wearing tiny bare-belly tees and tight shorts. One of them turned and gave him a broad smile. She had sun-streaked brown hair, green eyes, and a diamond stud in her right nostril.

"Hey," she said as if she knew him. Her girlfriends now turned and smiled at him as well.

"Hi," Kai answered a bit uncertainly. He thought she looked familiar, but he couldn't imagine where he could have known her from.

"Fairport Surf, remember?" the green-eyed young woman said. "You asked me about that yellow Rennie Yater board."

Now Kai remembered. She worked in the surf shop in Fairport where Kai had seen the Yater, which looked very similar to one that had been stolen from Curtis Ames's shed a week earlier. "What's up?"

"Just looking for something to do," the

young woman said. "Fairport's dead at night. You know, all families with little kids. We thought maybe there'd be some action here."

"So what happened to that Yater?" Kai asked.

"It sold the next day," she said. "Nine hundred bucks used. Can you believe it?"

"Definitely," Kai said. New or used, the board was one superfine stick. "You didn't happen to find out where it came from, did you?"

"I asked Rick," she said. "He's the owner of the shop. He said he bought it from this guy."

"What guy?" Kai asked.

"He didn't know the guy's name. Only that he had long bleached-blond dreadlocks and drove a red Jeep."

"Did the guy happen to mention how he got the board?"

"Rick didn't say."

"Does your boss always buy great used surfboards from strangers?" Kai asked.

"He's pretty careful about that," she said. "The guy must've seemed okay. I've seen creepy people come in and try to sell Rick boards and he's told them to get lost. I don't think he'd take a board if he knew it was stolen."

"Even a Yater he could get cheap and make a lot of money on?" Kai pressed.

The young woman twirled her streaked hair around her finger. "Well . . . he does pay me off the books, so I guess it's possible."

She seemed uncomfortable discussing her boss's honesty, so Kai decided not the push the question any harder.

"You live around here?" the young woman asked.

"Sort of."

"Want to hang out with us tonight?" she asked.

"I would, but I gotta get back to work."

"Where?"

"T-shirt shop over on East Street."

"Oh, yeah?" She glanced at her friends. "Maybe we'll stop by later."

"You can if you want," Kai said. "But the owner doesn't like it when people hang around and don't buy anything."

"Then maybe we'll buy something," she said.

"I wouldn't," Kai answered. "At least not there."

The young woman frowned. "So, uh, what time do you get off work?"

"Around ten."

"Maybe we'll come by then."

"You know any other cute guys?" asked one of her friends.

Kai thought of Bean. While he wasn't exactly cute, and seemed kind of gawky, Kai had noticed that there was something about him girls liked. Booger, on the other hand, was too young for this crowd.

"Let's see what happens," Kai said.

"Great," said the girl with the streaked brown hair.

By now the line had moved inside the ice-cream shop. In the chill of the air-conditioning Kai realized a pair of cool eyes were on him. He turned and saw Shauna looking at him, and at the young women he'd been talking to. Kai waited while they ordered ice-cream cones and paid.

"See you later," the green-eyed girl said. She and her friends left the shop. Being next in line, Kai now came face-to-face with Shauna.

"'See you later'?" she repeated.

Kai lifted and dropped his right shoulder.

"Aren't they a little old for you?" Shauna asked.

Kai lifted and dropped his *left* shoulder.

"Cat got your tongue?"

"So what's good?" Kai asked, pointing at the tubs of ice cream under the glass counter.

Shauna rolled her eyes. "It's ice cream, Kai. It's *all* good."

Kai leaned forward against the glass counter and whispered, "I'm kind of broke."

Shauna's lips twisted into a wry smile. "You should have asked your girlfriends to treat you."

"Forgot," Kai said.

Shauna let out a big sigh. "Okay, what flavor?"

"Uh, vanilla with Reese's topping?"

"Wait for me on the sidewalk," she said, then turned to the next person in line. "Can I help you?"

Kai went back out to the sidewalk. With Fourth of July weekend approaching, the town was getting crowded. Families trekked up and down the sidewalks, and minivans and SUVs clogged the streets. Kai heard a honk. A long, black hearse stopped at the curb. Kai stuck his head in the passenger window. Bean was sitting behind the wheel. Booger was sitting next to him.

"Your dad let you out?" Bean asked.

"I'm cutting class," Kai answered. "What're you guys up to?"

"Looking for wood for the bonfire," Booger said.

"Why don't you have a town dump truck deliver it, like Lucas does?" Kai kidded him.

"Is that sick or what?" Bean asked.

"His dad pays for that wood," Booger said. "For everybody else, going out and finding the wood is part of the fun. Buzzy just buys a truckload."

"You know why, don't you?" Bean asked.

"Because Lucas and his friends can't be bothered?" Kai guessed.

"Not just that," Bean said. "If Buzzy Frank is gonna have a bonfire, then it's got to be the biggest bonfire."

For a fraction of a second Kai felt the urge to make sure their bonfire was bigger than Buzzy's this year. But that was stupid. It was exactly that kind of dumb competitive thinking that led to fights over surf breaks. If Buzzy Frank was so insecure that he had to have the biggest bonfire around, that was his problem.

"So when do we actually start building?" Kai asked.

"Probably tomorrow, once the wind blows the surf out," Bean said. "Waves are supposed to be good early. You gonna be out there giving Lucas grief?"

"I'm not giving anyone grief," Kai said. "I'm just surfing where I feel like surfing. Why don't you come with me tomorrow morning?"

"To Screamers?" Bean jerked his head at his long board on the rack he'd built into the back of the hearse. The rest of the back was half filled with scrap wood. "Sorry, dude, but I value this stick too much to see Sam run it over."

"That's not gonna happen," Kai said.

"What's not gonna happen?" Shauna asked, handing him a large vanilla cone covered with Reese's topping.

"Thanks, Shauna. You're the best," Kai said.

"I bet you say that to all the girls." She pretended to pout.

"No, only the ones who give me free ice cream," Kai said.

Shauna punched him hard in the shoulder.

"Ow!" Kai yelped. "Where'd you learn to hit like that?"

"Old boyfriends," Shauna said.

"Thanks for the warning," Kai said, rubbing his shoulder. "I'll make sure I don't become one."

"Hey," Booger said from inside the car. "Can I get free ice cream too?"

"Only if you can take a punch," Shauna said.

"Forget it, I'll get some at home," said Booger.

"Now that I've served my purpose, I guess I can go back into the shop," Shauna said, a bit sourly.

"Wait," said Kai.

"Yes?" Shauna brightened hopefully.

"Any of you ever see a guy around here with bleached-blond dreadlocks?"

Shauna's expression dimmed just as fast as it had brightened.

"I have," Bean said.

"What do you know about him?" Kai asked.

"Uh, mostly that he's got long bleached-blond dreadlocks. Only, they're not really blond. They're kind of this gold color."

"Goldilocks!" Booger said.

"But no three bears, or pigs," said Shauna.

"What *else* do you know about him?" Kai asked.

"That's about it," Bean said. "No, wait. I think he was at my high school prom. He's a deejay or something."

"Know where to find him?" Kai asked.

"Maybe the yellow pages. Sometimes those guys put up flyers on bulletin boards and stuff. You could try Blockbuster and a couple of places like that."

"Why do you want to find him?" Shauna asked.

"Because I think he may have sold one of Curtis's boards to the owner of Fairport Surf."

"The yellow Rennie Yater you were talking about a couple of weeks ago?" said Bean.

"That's the one," Kai said. "Listen, maybe you guys could do me a favor, okay? Ask around about this guy. Let me know if you hear anything."

"Go undercover?" Booger asked eagerly.

Bean groaned. "You go undercover, Boogs. The rest of us will just ask around."

By the time Kai got back to T-licious almost forty-five minutes had passed. He expected to catch hell from Pat, but he really didn't care. His father was all bark and no bite.

Kai only wished he'd figured that out sooner.

Walking down the sidewalk, Kai saw someone standing in front of the T-shirt shop with his arms crossed. At first he didn't think anything of it. Husbands and boyfriends often stood outside while the wives and girlfriends went in to shop. But then Kai took another look. Something wasn't right. Maybe it was the way the guy stood directly in front of the T-shirt shop door. And he didn't exactly look like a tourist, either. With his dusty boots and jeans, sleeveless black T-shirt and sweat-stained red bandanna around his head, he looked more like he'd just spent the day doing construction work.

Kai stopped by the shop's window and looked in. The lights were all on, but the place was empty. That was strange too. Either Sean or Pat usually stayed in sight of the cash register. Kai stepped toward the guy with the red bandanna.

"Store's closed," the guy said.

"It shouldn't be," Kai said.

"Oh, yeah?"

"I work here, so maybe you could let me in," said Kai.

The bandanna guy shook his head.

"Seriously, this is my dad's place," said Kai.

The bandanna guy tilted his head down and gave Kai a look. "That so?"

"Is there a problem?" Kai asked.

"Not no more," the guy said.

Inside, Sean came out into the store from the back room, followed quickly by Pat, whose hunched shoulders and deeply knit eyebrows indicated that he was ticked off big-time.

Out on the sidewalk, Kai said, "There's my dad."

The bandanna guy looked impassively through the window. He shrugged and didn't budge from in front of the door.

Kai considered his options. He could wait out there, or pretend to leave and circle around the block to the back door and try to go in that way. He'd just made his decision when someone else came into the front of the store from the back room. It was another construction-worker type, this one with a short black beard and wearing black jeans and a button-down work shirt with the sleeves torn off.

And behind him came Buzzy Frank.

Six

Buzzy Frank saw Kai through the window the same moment Kai saw him. He said something to the bearded construction worker in the sleeveless work shirt. The guy came to the front door and wagged his finger at Kai.

Kai went past the bandanna guy and into the store. "This your other son?" Buzzy asked Pat.

"For the time being," Pat muttered.

"You know why I'm here?" Buzzy asked Kai.

"EBF Realty?" Kai replied.

Buzzy's eyebrows rose. "Very good."

"What's the *E* stand for?" Kai asked.

"Elliot," Buzzy said.

"You two know each other?" Pat asked with a puzzled frown.

"We've seen each other around," Buzzy answered.

The lines in Pat's face deepened, as if he couldn't see how there could be a connection. Then he straightened up. "The surf shop?"

"There and other places," Buzzy said. He looked at his watch. "I'll be back in half an hour. And there better not be any trace of anyone living here."

He and the guy in the sleeveless work shirt left. The door banged shut. Inside the store, no one moved.

"Great," the Alien Frog Beast muttered. "Just friggin' great. You gotta wonder who shoved the pole up that guy's butt. Usually they find out you're living in the store, they give you a couple of days or till the end of the week to find another place to live. This dickhead gave us half an hour. You believe that? We've got thirty minutes to get out."

"Well, actually, it's more like twenty-eight minutes now," Sean pointed out.

"Shut up!" Pat suddenly barked.

Sean jumped and shivered like a frightened puppy.

"We being evicted?" Kai asked.

"Not quite," Pat said. "The store stays. That SOB just made me write out a rent check for the rest of the summer. *And* additional security for the phone and electric."

"So the store stays, but we can't stay in the store?" Kai guessed.

"That's right," Pat said. "The bastard knows better than to evict us and lose the rent on this place for the rest of the summer. He knows it's too late to find a new commercial tenant at this point, so he'll let us stay until the tourist season passes, and then it's good-bye." Kai's father looked at his watch. "In the meantime it's almost eight o'clock and I gotta find a place for us to stay tonight."

"How about the truck?" Sean asked.

"How about you shut your damn trap and let me think?" Pat snarled. He lit a cigarette, took a drag, and started to hack.

"I might know a place," Kai said.

"Where?" Pat wheezed, red-faced from coughing.

"That motel you pass coming into town."

"You crazy?" his father said. "It's high season. I ain't paying for no motel, especially in high season."

"This might not be so bad," Kai said. "It's the rundown pink place on the water. I know the owner."

Pat gave him a curious look. "First you knew that SOB Buzzy Frank. Now you know the owner of that motel. So what's it gonna cost?"

"I don't know," Kai said.

"Well, if you know the owner so good, maybe you can get us a deal."

Kai couldn't get over how cheap his father was. Big Chief Hockaloogie must have had thousands of dollars in cash stashed in safe-deposit boxes at banks all over the country. And even though he'd probably just had to pony up some pretty hefty dinero to Buzzy for rent, there had to be plenty to spare. But the guy was so tight with a buck you'd have to wedge his hand open with a pry bar.

"I'll see what I can do," Kai said.

Pat jerked his head toward the back. "Call him."

Kai went into the office and looked up the Driftwood's number in the phone book. He dialed it and counted eight rings before he hung up. He dialed it again and this time counted six rings. Here it was, the height of the tourist season and Curtis didn't even have a phone machine to take messages from would-be guests. Somehow, Kai wasn't surprised.

Pat and Sean came into the back room just as Kai hung up for the second time.

"Well?" Pat asked.

"Couldn't reach him," Kai said, "but I'm pretty sure we can stay there tonight."

"It's Fourth of July week," Pat said. "Every motel from here to the lighthouse is full. What makes you think your friend has room?"

"Because the waves haven't been that good," Kai answered.

Pat scowled. "You run over there and make sure it's okay while Mr. Megabrains and I pack up the bedding and clothes. If he's got room, give us a call and we'll come over."

For once Kai was glad to do Pat's bidding. He left the shop and headed for the Driftwood.

Seven

Kai walked down the sidewalk, passing couples and families out for an after-dinner stroll. From the distance came the random pops and bangs of fireworks being lit by people who couldn't quite wait for the Fourth. Sun Haven Surf, Buzzy Frank's big surf shop in the middle of town, closed every night at 8 P.M. As Kai passed the shop, the lights inside were going out and the employees were leaving. Jade, the beautiful curvy young woman who worked behind the front counter, stepped out onto the sidewalk. Kai stopped.

"Hey," she said, smiling warmly.

"How are you?" Kai asked.

Jade shrugged. "Okay. You?"

"Not bad."

"I thought you were usually still at work at this time of night," she said.

"Something came up."

Jade crossed her arms over her chest and glanced down the sidewalk and then back at Kai. "Want to do something?"

That caught Kai by surprise. "Last time I saw you, it looked like you were doing something with someone else."

Jade wrinkled her nose and made a face. "I had to send him on his way. He was way too possessive."

"I've got to take care of some things right now," Kai said. "Maybe another time, okay?"

"That would be nice," Jade said.

When Kai got to the Driftwood, the orange vacancy sign was flickering on and off. Kai went through the screen door to the office and rang the bell. He waited, but nobody came through the door behind the desk that connected the motel office to Curtis's apartment. Finally Kai went around the counter and knocked.

Still no answer, but Kai could hear music coming from inside. Not just any music either, guitar-crazed surf movie music. Kai knocked again. "Curtis, you in there?"

"That you, grom?" Curtis called from inside.

"Yeah."

"Well, don't just stand there banging, come on in."

Kai pushed open the door. The living room was dark except for the gray light from the TV barely illuminating Curtis, who reclined on the couch with his feet up on the coffee table and a bottle of Jack Daniel's clenched in his fist.

"What's cookin' good lookin'?" Curtis asked in his gravelly voice, his eyes never leaving the screen.

"I rang the bell," Kai said. "What if it'd been someone looking for a room?"

"They'd be out of luck."

"But the vacancy sign's on," Kai said.

Curtis took a gulp of JD. "What are you all of a sudden, my mother? I don't want to answer the damn bell, I won't answer the damn bell."

"Then shouldn't you turn off the vacancy sign?" Kai asked.

"Why would I do that?" Curtis grumbled. "I got empty rooms to rent."

Kai stared at him for a second. "You're not making sense."

"You want to see what don't make sense?" Curtis asked. "Come over here."

Kai stepped closer. Now he could see the TV screen. An old grainy color surf movie was playing. Clearly one made on a sixteen millimeter film camera and then transferred to videotape years later. A bunch of crew cut guys on big 1960s long boards were taking off on some major waves.

"Recognize it?" Curtis asked.

"Waimea Bay," Kai said. "But I don't know the movie."

"That's 'cause you never saw it," Curtis said. "This is just some outtakes Bruce Brown put together for his friends."

Bruce Brown was probably the most famous surf-movie maker ever. A pioneer in the form.

"There!" Curtis suddenly pointed at the screen and hit the pause button on the remote. The grainy color picture froze on two surfers just starting down from the lip of a monstrous twenty-five-foot wave. One of them was wearing white-and-black-striped trunks and squatting on his board with his arms out-stretched. He was stocky and broad and reminded Kai of a sumo wrestler.

"Greg Noll," Kai said.

"Right. And the other guy?"

Kai kneeled closer and squinted at the screen, then looked back at the shadowy form of Curtis on the couch. "No way."

"Oh, grommy, you better believe it." Curtis pressed the play button and the movie started again. Noll, nicknamed Da Bull and one of the most famous surfers in history, had caught the huge wave on an angle and skittered down the face on a diagonal from the upper right to the lower left. Meanwhile Curtis charged straight down the face. As Noll moved farther to the left, the cameraman had to make a choice between following him or staying with Curtis. The cameraman followed Noll and Curtis disappeared from the screen.

"Just one of my many little moments of surfing immortality," Curtis muttered, and took another swig from the bottle.

"How's it make you feel?" Kai asked.

"How's it make me feel?" Curtis repeated. "Like crap. Da Bull goes down in the history books. He's in all the movies, the documentaries—"

"Wait a minute," Kai said. "He's in the history books because he rode the biggest wave that had ever been ridden up to that time."

"Yup. I guess that's what you had to do. Risk your mortal soul for a wave. You know, surfin's been the love of my life, but I never saw any reason to die for it. Guess that was my downfall."

"Let me ask you a question," Kai said. "If you could do it all over again, would you have ridden the wave Noll rode?"

Curtis grinned. "Only if I knew I was gonna survive." He hit rewind and wound the shot back to the beginning, then ran it forward. Only after watching it again did he glance back at Kai. "So to what do I owe the pleasure of this visit?"

"I need a room," Kai said.

Curtis's eyebrows rose. "Got yourself a hot date?"

"More like an eviction notice," Kai said. "My dad and half brother too."

"Where are they?" Curtis asked.

"Waiting for a call from me."

Curtis reached to the coffee table and picked up a wireless phone and tossed it to him. Kai called Pat and told him it was okay to come over, then put the phone back down.

"So, how'd you get your sorry butts evicted?" Curtis asked.

Kai explained that they'd been sleeping in the shop in violation of the lease. "Turns out Buzzy Frank's our landlord. Or at least his company is."

"His company?" Curtis said. "Try compa*nies*. That's just one of 'em. Christ, Buzzy Friggin' Frank's got more companies than a sea urchin's got spines. Construction, real estate, housing, stores, offices. He probably owns half this goddamn town, and is trying to buy the other half. He's got a *vision,* you know. A friggin' *concept* of what Sun Haven's gonna be someday. Only it won't be called Sun Haven anymore. It'll be called Buzzy Land."

Kai couldn't help smirking.

"You know what this place'll be like if Buzzy gets his way?" Curtis said. "Socially antiseptic and economically germ free. You'll be able to eat off the friggin' sidewalks. Only the best stores. Only the best restaurants. Only the best hotels. Only the best people. You know what kind of people are the best kind of people, grommy?"

"The ones with the most money?"

"Smart little grom, aren't ya? Damn straight they're the ones with the most money. And when they come here to Buzzy Land, the more of it they spend, the more of it winds up in Buzzy Friggin' Frank's pocket. Which is just the way Buzzy Friggin' Frank wants it."

"But if he already owns the surf shop and all this property and companies, he must be doing pretty well," Kai said.

Curtis grinned. "Buzzy Friggin' Frank's doing way better than just pretty well, my grommy little friend. Buzzy Friggin'. Frank's the richest man in town. He's already got more money than he knows what to do with. Know the Simpsons? Well, Buzzy Friggin' Frank's our very own Mr. Burns."

"If he's got so much, why does he still want more?" Kai asked.

Curtis took another hit off his bottle. "You don't want me to get all philosophical on your butt, do ya, grommy?"

"Can you keep it simple?" Kai asked.

"I can try," Curtis said. "The short answer? Fear of death."

Kai frowned. "Buzzy Frank thinks if he gets rich enough he won't die?"

"Well, it ain't that conscious, if you know what I mean," Curtis said. "It's more of an irrational kinda thing. But yeah, that's what it all sort of boils down to, if you ask me."

"That why you drink?" Kai asked.

"Yeah, probably," Curtis said. "Probably why guys my age dye their hair and buy fast cars and chase younger women. Why ladies dye their hair and get face-lifts and boob jobs and all the crap they do with makeup. And it's sure as hell why people go to church on Sunday morning."

"Then what's the answer?" Kai asked.

"Answer?" Curtis grinned. "Ride the biggest, most dangerous wave ever and make sure they get it on film. Hell, grom, I don't know what the friggin' answer is. Except maybe that this is just the way it's supposed to be. Death's a part of life. It's natural for things to be born and live and die."

"What if you die before your time?" Kai asked.

"Who says when it's someone's time?" Curtis said.

"Like a mother who's got a kid who's too young to be on his own," Kai said.

"Well, that's probably what fathers are for," Curtis said.

"What if the father isn't around?" Kai asked. "Or he's around but he doesn't give a crap?"

Curtis studied Kai closely. "We're not talkin' philosophy anymore, are we? We're talkin' about someone we both know pretty darn well."

Kai nodded.

"Well, that kid's gonna have to grow up and get on with it faster than he planned," Curtis said. "But he's a good person and there'll be people around who'll recognize that and want to help."

They heard the desk bell in the office ring.

"Speak of the devil." Curtis hefted himself up off the couch, and he and Kai went out into the office. Pat and Sean were there, looking around. Pat had that sour expression on his face, as if the Driftwood was such a fleabag that even *he* wasn't sure he could bring himself to stay there.

"Evening, gentlemen," Curtis said. "How may I help you?"

Pat got right to the point. He nodded at Kai. "My son here says you might give us a deal on a room."

Curtis looked at Kai, and for a moment Kai feared Curtis might say something like what a fine young man he was or some such garbage like that. But Curtis looked back at

Pat and said, "Forty-five dollars a night."

"How about for a week?" Pat asked.

"Forty-five a night," said Curtis.

"How about a month?"

"Same thing," said Curtis.

"So where's the deal?" Pat asked.

"The deal, my good man, is that this is high season and from now until Labor Day you won't find a motel room within a hundred miles of here for less than a hundred eighty a night. So you're lookin' at a seventy-five percent discount off the going rate."

"Suppose we agree you don't have to give us clean sheets and towels every day," Pat said.

"You think for forty-five a night you get clean sheets and towels every day?" Curtis asked. "For that price you should be thankful you get a sheet or towel, period."

Pat's sour look got even more sour. "What kind of place is this, anyway?"

"I kind of think it's the only place left for you," Curtis said. "Now, I've enjoyed our little chat, gentlemen, but right now I feel I'd like to spend the rest of the evening with my good friend, Mr. Jack Daniel's, so if you would be so kind as to make up your mind I'll be able to shut off the lights, lock the door, and return to my reflections on immortality."

Pat frowned. "Okay, we'll take a room for a night and see how it goes," he said, as if he were doing Curtis some huge favor.

"That'll be forty-five dollars," Curtis said.

"People usually pay at check out," Pat complained.

"Well, I don't conduct business as usual around here, my good man," Curtis replied. "I deal strictly on a take it or leave it basis."

Muttering to himself, Pat reached into his pocket and pulled out a wad of bills. He peeled off two twenties and a five and slid them across the counter to Curtis, who handed Pat a key attached to a blue plastic diamond with the number 22 on it.

"Have a pleasant evening, gentlemen." Curtis limped through the door, back into his living room.

Room 22 was around the back of the motel and on the second floor. Kai and Sean followed Pat to the truck to get some clothes, then walked around behind the motel to climb the outside stairs. Pat stopped when he saw all the surfboards scattered around the backyard.

"This where you got that surfboard of yours?" he asked Kai.

"Uh-huh."

"Why doesn't he sell 'em?"

"He doesn't want to," Kai answered, knowing his father would never be able to understand that.

They climbed the stairs to the second floor. Pat and Sean went ahead, but Kai paused by the rail and looked out at the dark inky ocean and the star-filled sky. It was a beautiful view and Kai understood why Curtis would have a difficult time leaving. A bottle rocket shot up into the dark from the beach and exploded with a flash of light. Kai turned and went down to the room.

"What a dump," Pat was saying as Kai entered and pulled the door closed behind him to stop all the bugs from streaming in toward the light. Having just spent a month sleeping on the floor of the back room at the T-shirt shop, Kai found it amusing that Pat could be so critical of a room that actually had beds. On the other hand, he had to admit that his father was at least partly right. Thin brown cigarette burns scarred every piece of furniture and flat surface. Even the blankets on the beds had brown-rimmed burn holes in them.

The room had two queen-size beds. Pat flopped down on one of them without bothering to take off his shoes, picked up the TV remote and started to watch. It would be up to Sean and Kai to figure out who got the other bed. Kai was tired and knew at that point he could sleep anywhere.

"You take the bed," he told his half brother. "I'll go back down and get one of the rafts. I'll have no trouble sleeping on that tonight."

"Thanks." Sean sat down on the other bed.

Kai went back outside and down to the truck, and he got one of the inflatable rafts. Once again he climbed the outside stairs to the second floor and paused by the railing to look out at the ocean. It was late and quiet now, and he could hear the waves crashing on the beach and smell the salt air. A large sailboat moved slowly along the horizon, the bow, stern, and mast lights forming a triangle. Except for the past two years, Kai had spent his entire life near the ocean. Maybe he'd needed those past two inland years to understand. But now he knew he would never lose sight of the ocean again.

Eight

Kai was up early the next morning. Even in the gray predawn the air had a moist warm quality, and he could tell it was going to be a hot day. He walked to T-licious to get his board and wet suit. Were it not for the fact that he'd be surfing just after dawn, he probably wouldn't have needed the wet suit at all.

From the T-shirt shop he headed down to the beach. The surf was okay again, mostly knee to waist high. The sun was just peeking over the horizon. Lucas and Buzzy had gotten there ahead of him and were now paddling out. Down the beach, Lucas's pile of scrap wood had grown huge. Kai could only assume that Buzzy had purchased a second truckload and had it delivered the previous afternoon. Up and down the beach were other piles of wood or half-built bonfires. None would come close to the size of Buzzy's.

Kai put his board down on the sand and kneeled beside it. It was one of those days when he wasn't in a rush to get into the water. The waves were small and sectiony and Kai didn't mind staying on the beach a few moments longer than usual, taking his time as he rubbed wax onto the deck of his new board.

He heard a car door bang shut. In the lot on the other side of the boardwalk, he could see the top of Bean's head. A few moments later Bean, Shauna, and Booger crossed the boardwalk. Old #43 was too heavy for Shauna to carry all the way from her house each day, so Bean was keeping it in the hearse for her.

Booger sat down on the sand and slipped his fins on. "Where're we surfing today?"

"I'm surfing Screamers," Kai answered. "And you guys are welcome to join me."

The others didn't say a word.

"I can pretty much guarantee you Lucas and his crew will leave you alone," Kai added.

"I'll stick with Sewers, thanks," Booger

said, heading for the water with his body-board.

Bean and Shauna waxed their boards. Being a beginner, Shauna was probably better off in the slower, softer waves at Sewers. As far as Bean was concerned, it was obvious that no matter what Kai said, he was still uncomfortable with Lucas and his crew.

"Can you guys help me with something?" Shauna asked. "I keep having this problem. Sometimes I try to pop up and my hands slip off the rail."

"Wax helps," Bean half teased.

"I wax the rails and that helps for a while," Shauna said, "but then they get slippery again."

"Let's see the wax you're using," Kai said. Shauna handed him a half-used white rectangular bar. Kai scraped it with his thumbnail.

"It's probably too soft," Kai said, handing it back to her.

"It was fine last week," Shauna said.

"The water temperature's gone up a couple of degrees, and with how hot and sunny it's been getting, you're probably rubbing this stuff off faster than you think." Kai handed her the rest of his bar. "When you finish surfing today, let the sun melt the old wax off. Then try this stuff. It's a bit harder and shouldn't come off as fast."

"Thanks."

Kai stood up and tucked his board under his arm. "Sure you guys don't want to come over to Screamers?"

"Why don't you surf Sewers with us today?" Shauna asked.

Kai raised the tip of his board. "On a day like today Screamers is the only place where I'll get any kind of ride on this thing."

"Well, have fun."

Kai walked down the beach to the channel along the jetty and paddled out. When he got outside, neither Lucas nor Buzzy nodded or said anything. Instead they focused on Lucas's surfing. Today he was working on something that involved going backside and doing a tail slide, with Buzzy urging Lucas to keep trying no matter how weak the wave. The more Kai saw of Buzzy, the more he saw a man who insisted on having everything his way.

Kai caught a few waves, but found them weak and mushy. Sets were coming in less and less frequently. For no particular reason he decided to paddle farther out, well past the breaking waves, to see what Sun Haven looked like from the water. He got out into the blue water and turned around. While neither Buzzy nor Lucas would look at him before, both now shot him curious glances, as if they couldn't figure out what he was doing out there.

Meanwhile, Kai began to see what Curtis had meant about Buzzy Land. The whole shoreline was private houses and, except for the Driftwood Motel, fancy hotels and resorts. Kai didn't doubt that Curtis was serious when he said his was the only motel within a hundred miles that charged less than one hundred and eighty dollars a night during the summer.

Just then something black appeared in the water beneath him.

Nine

For a split second Kai's heart jumped into his throat. Ever since Bethany Hamilton lost her arm to a fifteen-foot tiger shark back in Hanalei, he'd been acutely aware of things in the water beneath him. But this was just a black plastic bag. These days the ocean was filled with them.

Kai started to paddle back in. By now more of Lucas's crew had arrived for the morning session. There were even a couple of new kids Kai had never seen before. Since the waves weren't worth fighting for, Kai didn't see the point in hassling with them, and he paddled toward Sewers instead. A little while later he joined Booger, Bean, and Shauna on the outside.

"Not much of a day, huh?" Bean said, sitting on his board.

"Beats working," said Kai. He turned to Shauna. "How's it going?"

"Great," she said. "The only thing I don't get is why when I catch a wave, I always go straight toward shore, but when you guys catch a wave you go sideways."

Instead of answering, Kai looked out to see what was coming in. A smallish set was on the way. "Let's see what you're doing," Kai said. "Maybe you could take one of these waves."

"Okay." Shauna got prone on her board and started to paddle without really watching the wave behind her. She managed to catch it, then got to one knee as it closed out. For a second Kai thought she was going to eat it in the suds, but she held on and rose to both feet and rode the rest of the way in.

Kai turned to Bean and gave him a questioning look.

"I counted at least four, maybe five major mistakes," Bean said. "How about you?"

"Something like that," Kai replied. "You want to tell her?"

"No way," Bean said. "She asked you, not

me. In fact"——he turned his board around and started to paddle——"I think this is a good time to catch a wave myself." With a few almost effortless paddles, he caught a wave.

Chicken, Kai thought with a smile while Bean rode down the line, walking his long board like a dancer. By now Booger had paddled out on his bodyboard.

"About that guy you're looking for with blond dreadlocks and a red Jeep," he said. "I was thinking . . . I bought some turntables and a mixer from a guy last year. He had *brown* dreadlocks. I think he was driving an old beat-up BMW."

"How'd you find him?" Kai asked.

"He posted an ad in the music store in town."

"He was from around here?"

"Yeah, I'm pretty sure," Booger said. "Maybe a town or two over. It had to be a cash deal. No checks or money orders. Funny thing was, he brought the turntables over to my house, you know? Like he had all this stuff in the backseat of his car. So I paid him, and he asks me if I'm interested in anything else, and I'm like, what've you got? He opened the car's trunk and it's like a fricken miniwarehouse.

He's got brand-new MP3 players still in the box, cell phones, a couple of electric guitars, boom boxes . . . You know my carve board? That's where I got it. He had three of them packed in there. And get this. He says if there's something I didn't see that I want, he can probably get it for me."

"You remember his name, phone number, anything?" Kai asked.

Booger shook his head. "Tell you the truth, dude, the whole thing kind of freaked me. Like what if all this stuff was hot? And the way he acted was like . . . I had this feeling that if I'd asked him for a Glock nine he probably would have said 'No sweat.' I just wanted him to go away and never come back."

"Okay, thanks for telling me."

"I mean, it might not even be the same guy," Booger said.

"Hard to say," Kai replied.

A small wave jacked up behind them. "I'm going. See ya." Booger kicked into the wave.

Kai waited outside. A guy who had brown dreadlocks last year could have bleached them blond, or gold, this year. Could have sold the old BMW and gotten a Jeep too. Shauna got back out and sat up on her board next to him.

"Did you see?" she said. "It's always the same. I catch the wave, but all I can ever do is ride it straight in."

"There are some things you could do differently," Kai said.

"Like what?"

"Well, first of all, you should be looking over your shoulder as you paddle, so you can position yourself for the wave. It would help a lot if, instead of lying flat on the board, you arched your back. That makes it easier to look behind you. And at your stage you don't really want to catch the wave at the peak. You're better off on the shoulder. And since these waves aren't very big or fast, you could take off on an angle so that you're already a little bit turned into the wave. And you're not really popping up. You're just getting to your knees and waiting, then standing up. That's a bad habit. You're better off learning to pop right up."

"Is that all?" Shauna pouted.

"Hey, you asked," Kai said.

"Okay," she said. "Arch back, look behind, take off on the shoulder on an angle, pop right up. No knees. Piece of cake."

"Give it a shot," Kai said.

A small wave was coming. Shauna started paddling and looked over her shoulder to position herself. She angled the board, caught the wave, and promptly rolled over sideways.

A moment later her head popped out of the suds. She grabbed her board and gave her head a shake, sending a spray in the air, climbed on and started to paddle back. Meanwhile Kai looked at the shore. That strange, twitchy guy from the other morning was back, standing at the water's edge, looking out at them. Even from a hundred yards out in the water, Kai could see him hopping up and down, his head rolling and snapping, his hands fluttering as if he couldn't control them.

Shauna paddled out beside him.

"You ever see that guy before?" Kai asked her.

"No, but I'm pretty new around here," she said. "What's wrong with him?"

"I don't know," Kai said. "He came up to me the other day on the beach acting really strange. It was like he was trying to talk, but all he could do was make these weird sounds."

"Maybe he's, like, got something wrong with him," Shauna said.

"That's what I was thinking," Kai said.

"Makes you wonder if he should be alone on the beach."

They were both quiet for a moment. Then Shauna said, "So what did I do wrong that time?"

"A little too much angle on your takeoff," Kai said. "Try for a little less next time."

They waited for the next half decent wave to come in. Kai swung his head back and forth, looking for a wave, then looking at the strange guy on the beach. A wave came and this time Shauna caught the shoulder with a little less of an angle. It looked like she was about to pop up when she lost her balance and fell.

Back in the soup again.

But this time when her head popped up, she had a big grin. Kai waited while she got on her board and paddled back out.

"I felt it!" she said excitedly. "I really did! Like for a second I was actually going sideways in the curl! It was so cool!"

"What happened?"

"I tried to get up and the water just ripped my hand off the rail and I fell."

"You gotta keep your hands off the rail," Kai said. "Try planting them flat on the deck when you pop up. Kind of like doing a push up."

By now Bean and Booger had come back out.

"Guys, watch this!" Shauna said eagerly. Another wave was coming and she started to paddle into position.

"How's it going?" Bean asked Kai while they watched Shauna dig for the wave.

"She's getting there," Kai said.

Shauna caught the wave at an angle, planted her hands on the deck of the board, popped up and instantly did a header right into the trough.

"Big improvement," Bean quipped.

"Give her some time," Kai said. He looked back at the beach. The strange guy was still standing at the waterline. "You guys know who that is?"

"That's Spazzy," Booger said. "He and his sister come here every summer."

"What's the story?" Kai asked.

"I don't know. People say the wiring in his head is messed up."

Kai was about to look back to see what Shauna was doing when he saw one of the guys from Lucas's crew walking out of the water and up onto the beach with his board. It was Runt, the red-haired kid who always tried to act so tough. Runt put his board down and started to walk toward the weird guy.

Maybe it was the agro posture of Runt's body, or the expression on his face. But something told Kai that there was going to be trouble.

Ten

Without waiting for a wave, Kai started to paddle in. That weird guy, Spazzy, or whatever they called him, had seen Runt by now and was starting to back away up the beach. Meanwhile Runt bent down and picked something up from the sand like he was going to throw it.

Aw, crap. Kai truly couldn't believe what he was seeing. Garbage like this wasn't supposed to happen in real life. It only happened in those dumb made-for-school movies about bullying that everyone felt compelled to show ever since those two nutcases went berserk at Columbine.

The spazzy guy started to back away faster

now, stumbling and almost losing his balance as he turned to run. Runt wound up, and threw whatever he'd picked up. Because of the way the spazzy guy was jerking and flailing, Kai couldn't tell if anything hit him or not.

"Get the hell outa here, you freak!" Runt shouted, and bent down to pick up something else to hurl. Kai reached the shallows and jumped off his board. He ripped the leash off his ankle, tore up the beach, and blindsided Runt just as he was about to throw.

They both went down. Kai had the advantage, since Runt didn't know what had hit him. But now he had to wrestle him in the sand. Of course, Runt had to fight back, so they rolled around, Kai getting sand in his mouth and eyes before he managed to grab Runt's arm, twist it around his back, and force him facedown in the sand.

"Leggo!" Runt tried to fight loose.

"Just chill," Kai said, holding him down, but not hurting him. He spit the sand out of his mouth and tried to blink it out of his eyes.

"Let go!" Runt kept struggling.

Kai twisted the kid's arm up behind his back a little more. Runt yelped, then laid still.

"What's your problem?" Kai asked.

"Fuck you, what's *your* problem?" Runt growled back.

"I don't have a problem," Kai said. "And I'm not the one throwing stuff at retards."

"I'm not a retard," someone said.

Kai swiveled his head around in surprise. The spazzy guy was standing there, blinking, licking his lips, jerking around like someone was zapping him with a stun gun. Yet the words had been spoken with perfect clarity. Kai stared at him, totally confused.

"I have Tourette's syndrome," the guy said.

Whatever it was, Kai had never heard of it. Runt squirmed again. Kai let go and stood up. Runt leaped to his feet, spitting sand out of his mouth and scratching it out of his hair. He brought up his fists like he still wanted to fight.

"You want to go at it? Come on, let's go!" Runt danced around, waving his fists, ducking and weaving like he was in the first round of a heavyweight fight. Kai and the spazzy guy glanced at each other and the spazzy guy actually smiled, as if he agreed with Kai that Runt was a couple of french fries short of a Happy Meal.

"Look, just go away, okay?" Kai said. "And don't throw stuff at people."

"You chicken?" Runt spit and waved his fists. "They call you tuna, right? Chicken of the sea."

Without warning, Kai brought his fist back and took a quick step toward the kid.

"Ah!" Caught by surprise, Runt yelped and jumped back out of range.

Kai smiled. "Yeah, I'm chicken. And what's wrong with you? Why can't you leave people alone?"

Runt dropped his fists and looked confused. He pointed a finger at the spazzy guy. "What's wrong with him?"

By now Lucas and his crew had come ashore, including the new guy with the tattoos and piercings. Bean and Booger came in too.

"What's going on?" Lucas asked.

"Maybe you could find Runt a bone to gnaw on," Kai said. "He's definitely got a lot of energy to burn."

"Screw you," Runt snarled.

Sam took a step toward Kai. "What are you? The protector of weirdos or something?" Clearly he meant to include Bean and Booger as well.

Kai sighed. He was tempted to ask Sam if he was absent the day they handed out brains, but it would only create more antagonism. Instead he turned to Lucas. "Just call off your dogs, okay? Then tonight we can meet in the alley with chains and knives and settle this like real men."

"I'll be there," Runt said.

Even Lucas had to roll his eyes. "Runt, you idiot, he wasn't serious."

"Huh?" Runt looked even more confused.

Lucas turned back to Kai. "The real place to settle this would be in the waves. Like in Fairport in a few weeks. Oh, wait, I forgot. You're the big soul surfer who's completely anticompetition. Just like your hero, Duke Kahana-what's-his-face, the great ambassador of surfing. You know, it's funny. I read up on that guy and guess what? He wasn't against competition at all. In fact, he was a totally competitive animal."

Kai felt a frown form on his face, but he knew better than to argue.

"Want to know how the great ambassador of surfing got to travel around the world putting on surf demonstrations?" Lucas continued. "Because he was a competitive swimmer and he was being invited to swimming meets. In fact, he was so competitive he won gold medals in two Olympics. My guess is that he would have been the first one to sign up for a surfing heat, only they didn't have any back then. So I think you should come up with another excuse for not competing, dude, because if the big Duke was around today, I'm pretty sure he'd be looking forward to Fairport."

Lucas turned and walked away, and his crew followed him, except the guy with piercings and tattoos, who gave Kai a long look as if he was sizing him up. Kai couldn't read the guy's expression. But something about him was really troubling. Finally he turned and left too.

Eleven

"**I** think that's true," said Spazzy, blinking and jerking again.

Kai looked at him curiously.

"I, I read it in a book," Spazzy said. He started to hop up and down. "And thanks for helping me before."

Kai watched him hop like he was on an invisible pogo stick.

"I saw you surfing Screamers," Spazzy said. "But you're not one of them. Why did they let you?"

"Welcome to the Screamers Liberation Front," Bean said. "We who are fighting for the cause of liberating Screamers from the neoprene grip of tyranny."

"What's your name?" Booger asked.

"Caleb Winthrop. But everyone around here calls me Spazzy. If you said Caleb I might not know you meant me."

"Doesn't it bother you when people call you that?" Bean asked.

Spazzy moved his head back and forth. It was very strange to Kai how at some moments Spazzy's body appeared to be completely out of his control, but at other moments he could appear, briefly, calm and normal.

"I spend most of the year at this school in Santa Barbara. It's for people like me. The first thing they teach you is not to take anything people do or say personally." Spazzy licked the back of his hand, then sniffed it, then licked it again and sniffed it again. "I mean, when you do the kind of stuff I do, you *better* learn not to take what people say personally."

"Can you ever control it?" Kai asked.

"Sometimes. Like for a really short time, but then it just builds up inside you and what comes out is even weirder than usual. So they teach you to relax and let whatever happens just happen. Like the other day when I came up to you on the beach and made all those stupid screechy noises? It's because I got all excited and nervous and was trying to be cool and calm."

"Wait a minute," Bean said. "Is this the thing where some people curse like crazy and can't stop themselves?"

"Sometimes," said Spazzy. "That's called coprolalia and not all Tourette's patients have it. My friend Ray has it and when he really gets wound up, it's like, totally crazed. Like this one time we went to the movies and there was this ridiculously long line to get in and our movie was gonna start at any moment and Ray went off cursing like a madman. Like he couldn't help it, but everybody freaked and the place just cleared out. Next thing you know, we're first in line." Spazzy grinned proudly.

"But what about once you're in the movie?" Bean said. "Doesn't he bother everyone?"

"We usually try to go to heavy-action R-rated stuff and sit in the back. When Ray goes off most of the audience probably thinks it's part of the sound track."

Kai chuckled. Spazzy was a cool guy.

Spazzy stared at something over Kai's shoulder, and immediately started blinking and twitching again. Kai turned. A serious-looking young woman was taking determined strides across the beach toward them. She was wearing neatly pressed blue slacks, a white sweater, and what looked from a distance like pearl earrings and a pearl necklace. They seemed like the kind of clothes a sixty-year-old woman might wear, not someone in their early twenties. And it was hard to imagine anyone at any age dressing like that at eight in the morning.

"Aw, crap, it's the Wicked Witch of the West." Spazzy started across the beach to meet her, as if he didn't want her to mix with Kai and his friends. She stopped and crossed her arms. Kai couldn't hear what she said, but it looked like she was scolding him. Spazzy hop-walked past her as if he didn't want to hear it.

"Can someone explain to me what just happened?" Bean said.

"I think we just met Spazzy, and he seems like a cool guy," Kai said.

"What's Santa Barbara?" Booger asked.

"A place in California," Bean said.

"What's he doing here?" Booger asked.

"Maybe you should ask him sometime," Kai said.

"He said something about Screamers," Bean

said. "But how would he even know about Screamers?"

"Why are you guys asking me this stuff?" Kai said. "I just met him too."

"Weird," said Booger.

They watched Spazzy walk back up the beach, followed by the well-dressed young woman. Then they turned and watched Lucas and his crew paddling back out to Screamers.

"What do you want to do?" asked Booger.

Bean checked his watch, then looked back at the waves. "Surf. What else?"

They turned back toward the water. Kai let Booger go ahead, then said, "Hey, Bean."

Bean had just put on his leash. Now he straightened up. "Yeah?"

"Who's the new guy in Lucas's crew?"

Bean didn't even have to look to know who Kai was talking about. "Derek."

"What's his story?"

"You don't want to know."

Twelve

Kai surfed until 9 A.M., and headed back to the Driftwood to shower and change. Then he left the motel room and went back down the outside stairs, planning to grab some breakfast before going to the T-shirt shop. As he walked around the side of the motel he saw Curtis standing in the parking lot with two men wearing slacks, short-sleeved shirts, and ties. Both men had pocket protectors loaded with pens and mechanical pencils. Curtis was reading a pink sheet of paper one of the men had just handed him.

He looked back up at the two men. "Where'd you say you were from?"

"Town engineer's office," one of the men answered.

"And you're citing me for creating an environmental hazard?" Curtis said. "What the hell are you talking about?"

"It's right over here, Mr. Ames." One of the men led him over to the green garbage Dumpster in the corner of the parking lot near the street. The man took a pen from his pocket protector and pointed at a thin dribble of smelly yellowish liquid that dripped out of the bottom of the Dumpster and snaked down the driveway, along the curb and disappeared into a storm sewer in the street.

"Yer shittin' me," Curtis sputtered in disbelief.

"No, Mr. Ames, I'm afraid we're not, er, doing that," the man replied. "Town ordinance clearly states that it is the responsibility of every home and business owner to make sure that he prevents undesirable effluence from entering the city sewer system from his personal or business property."

Curtis waved the pink piece of paper at them. "Well, then I expect that if I go down to city hall I'll find records of citations of every goddamn business and homeowner in this town who ever spread chemical fertilizer or weed killer or bug fucker on their lawns, right?

Because we all know goddamn well that every time it rains all that shit goes right down the sewer and out into the ocean, where it's already killed off the entire population of local lobsters, and it's in the process of killing ninety percent of the world's living reefs, not to mention feeding red tides and freakish algae blooms and more or less destroying the last great natural resources on this great cesspool of a planet we call Earth."

"All I can tell you, Mr. Ames, is that we do cite polluters whenever we can find them," one of the men said. There was something odd about both men. Kai realized their upper torsos looked thick and out of proportion to their heads and lower bodies. One of them kept dabbing his forehead with a handkerchief. It was definitely hot out, but not *that* hot.

Curtis held up the pink sheet before their eyes and began to tear it into little pieces. "Who put you up to this? How much did they pay ya to come out here and hassle me with this shit?"

"Uh, sir, by tearing up that citation I'm afraid you will be found in contempt," one of the men said.

"Contempt? You want to see contempt?

I'll show you contempt." Curtis spun around and stomped toward the motel office.

Kai had a bad feeling about what was about to happen. He quickly followed Curtis inside. The door from the office to Curtis's living room was open and Kai could hear Curtis banging around as if he was looking for something while he muttered, "Contempt, huh? I'll show those petty bureaucratic lightweights what contempt looks like."

Kai heard the sound of a breech opening and clacking shut. He stepped through the door and closed it behind him. Curtis was standing in the middle of the living room with his sawed-off shotgun in his hands.

"Curtis, don't," Kai said.

The older man jerked his head around. "What are you doing here?"

"Saving your ass."

"Sorry, grommet, it's too late for that," Curtis growled. "This is the last straw. I've had it with this crap. I'm renaming this place the Alamo. The only way they'll take me out is in a body bag."

"And they will, too," Kai said. "You walk out there with that gun and you'll be doing exactly what they want you to do."

Curtis frowned.

"Come here." Kai went to the window and parted the blinds slightly. "Look at those guys. See anything?"

"Yeah, I see a couple of geeks from the town engineer's office. So what?"

"Look at their chests," Kai said.

Curtis squinted through the blinds. He frowned. "What the hell?"

"Kevlar vests. Body armor. Not exactly the normal dress code for geeks from the town engineer's office, is it?"

"Well, I'll be," Curtis muttered.

"That means they expect you to go out there and do something crazy," Kai said. "Want to know what they don't expect? They don't expect you to go back out there and apologize for tearing up that citation. Say it was temporary insanity and ask for another one."

Curtis grit his teeth. "The hell I will."

"Why are you trying to make trouble for yourself?" Kai asked. "Know how easy it would be to fix your problem? All you have to do is move the Dumpster. Maybe you don't even have to move it. Maybe all you have to do is put a bucket under the leak. But if you don't go back out there, they're going to have this contempt thing hanging over your head. I don't know exactly what that means, but I'm pretty sure you can't fix it with a bucket."

Curtis pursed his lips and looked down at the floor. His shoulders drooped. "Christ on broken crutches."

Kai waited and said nothing. Finally Curtis heaved a big sigh. "You're a smart kid, grom, but you're missing the big picture. Maybe you're right about this battle, but the war ain't over. They're gonna keep coming back at me again and again. They're grinding me down, grom. It's like they know I can only take so much of this before I blow."

"Maybe something will change," Kai said. "Maybe you'll be able to stop it once and for all."

"Not a chance," Curtis said. "It's me against the world, grom. There's too much money to be made by booting my sorry ass out of here. Greed's a powerful force, my friend. If it was a wave, it would be twice the size of Maverick's going off twenty-four-seven, three hundred sixty-five days a year."

"Okay, but for right now you could make your life a lot easier by putting down the shotgun and going back out there and asking for another copy of that citation," Kai said.

Curtis looked down at the gun, then tossed it onto the couch. Kai flinched. It was crazy the way he tossed that gun around. Like he didn't care that it might go off accidentally.

"Okay, grom, this time I'll do it," Curtis said. "But I'm making no promises about next time."

Thirteen

When Kai got to the T-shirt shop he found the Alien Frog Beast Hockaloogie standing on the sidewalk outside, staring at the window.

"This surfing display ain't working." Kai's father was talking about a display he'd asked Kai to create after he'd noticed that the only store in town that seemed to get foot traffic on hot sunny afternoons was Sun Haven Surf. The reason people went into the surf shop at that time of day was that in the afternoons the onshore breeze would start to blow out the waves. The surfers had nothing better to do than look at surfboards and ogle Jade, Kai's sexy "friend" who worked behind the front counter. Pat figured that if he had Kai do a surfing display for T-licious, he might be able to sell a few T-shirts to those surfers, but Kai, who hated the scams his father pulled on people, made the display as ugly as possible by featuring T-shirts with pigs and ducks on surfboards.

"So what do you want to do?" Kai asked his father.

"How else do they get surfer kids to shop?" the Alien Frog Beast asked.

Kai thought of suggesting that his father hire a sexy girl like Jade to work the counter, but that was out of the question. Instead he said, "You could become a sponsor."

"How's that work?" Pat asked.

"Usually you pick out the hottest, coolest surfer around and the store gives him some free stuff," Kai said. "In return, the surfer puts the store's logo on his boards and maybe on his wet suit. Other kids see the cool surfer wearing the store's stuff and they want to wear it also."

"So you gotta have some kind of logo?" Pat looked unhappy.

"It's pretty key," Kai said. He figured that would be the end of the conversation. Any idea that involved Pat giving away anything for free, not to mention actually *paying* for someone to design a logo, would pretty much blow the deal clear out of the water.

"There he is!" someone suddenly said.

Kai and his father looked down the sidewalk where a man was pointing at them. It was Mr. Asoki, the tourist Pat had scammed the night before. With him was a man wearing a green plaid sports jacket and slacks.

"Crap!" Pat grumbled and dashed into the store.

Meanwhile Mr. Asoki and the man in the sports jacket came toward Kai. Mr. Asoki was clearly excited. "He charge me seventy-five dollar a shirt!" he was telling the man in the green plaid jacket. "In other store same shirt twenty-two dollar."

Kai stayed on the sidewalk. As Mr. Asoki approached, his eyes fixed on Kai and he pointed at him. "Him. He work there too."

The man in the plaid jacket stopped. "You work in this shop, son?"

Kai nodded. By now, other people on the sidewalk had stopped to see what the commotion was about.

"Why don't we go inside and talk this over," said the man in the plaid jacket.

They went in. Not surprisingly, Sean and Pat had vanished. The man in the plaid jacket turned to Kai. "Would you ask the older gentleman to come out, please?"

Kai went into the back room. It was empty and the back door was slightly ajar, allowing a thin slice of sunlight in. Pat and Sean had bailed. Kai pulled the door closed and went out front again. Mr. Asoki and the man in the plaid jacket were waiting by the counter.

"They're gone," Kai said.

The man in the plaid jacket didn't seem surprised to hear that. He held out his hand. "I'm Eric Blake, with the Sun Haven Chamber of Commerce. And you're?"

"Kai." They shook hands.

"Just Kai?" Mr. Blake asked.

Kai tried to remember which *South Park* character's last name Pat was using this time. "Garrison."

"Well, Kai, it seems Mr. Asoki has a problem with what you charged him for his shirts," Mr. Blake said. "Mr. Asoki, can we see that receipt?"

Mr. Asoki handed the credit card receipt for the shirts to Mr. Blake, who turned it over to Kai. "Mr. Asoki has discovered that other shops in town will sell him the same shirt for considerably less."

"Twenty-two dollar," Mr. Asoki said.

"Seventy-five dollars a shirt seems a little extreme, don't you think?" Mr. Blake asked.

"Sure does," said Kai. "Must be a mistake."

"One that I imagine you can correct very easily," Mr. Blake said, tilting his head toward the cash register.

Kai opened the cash register. Twenty-two times four was eighty-eight. Three hundred minus eighty-eight was two hundred and twelve dollars. Kai counted out ten twenties, one ten, and two ones and handed them to Mr. Asoki. "I'm sorry about that, sir."

"Well, Mr. Asoki," Mr. Blake said, "I hope that helps remedy your problem." He reached into his jacket pocket and pulled out a light blue certificate. "In addition, for your trouble I'd like you to have this gift certificate to my restaurant, the Lobster House. I'd like you and your family to have a free dinner on behalf of the citizens of Sun Haven."

"Thank you very much, sir," Mr. Asoki said. "Thank you."

"And thank you for bringing your family here to Sun Haven," Mr. Blake said. "I hope you will tell all your friends about your very pleasant visit to our town."

"I will, thank you." Mr. Asoki left the store. Mr. Blake didn't.

Fourteen

"Kai Garrison." Mr. Blake placed the elbows of his plaid jacket on the glass counter and leaned toward Kai, holding him steady in his eyes. "Where're you from, Kai?"

"No particular place," Kai answered.

"Here and there?" Mr. Blake guessed. "Move around a lot?"

Kai nodded.

"Change your name about as often as you change your address?"

Kai didn't answer.

"You know, Kai, many of us who live here in Sun Haven take a great deal of pride in our little town. We like to think that when people come here to visit they have a good time and they get what they pay for. They leave Sun Haven with smiles on their faces and fond memories that they share with their friends, so that the following year, their friends might want to come here as well. Now you may be surprised to hear this, Kai, but even before Mr. Asoki came to my office today, I'd been hearing rumors that there might be a problem at this particular location. Actually, I bet you're not surprised to hear that, are you?"

Kai shook his head.

Eric Blake had not taken his eyes off Kai, nor had Kai taken his away from Blake. If this was a staring contest, Kai had no trouble playing. Blake raised one eyebrow and glanced toward the door that led to the back room.

"Your friends really gone, Kai?" he asked. "Or are they back there waiting for me to leave?"

"They're gone. You're welcome to go back there and see for yourself."

"No, thanks, I believe you," Mr. Blake said. "So the older gentleman, he saw trouble coming and he ran, leaving you behind to deal with it. How old are you, Kai?"

"Fifteen."

"Little young to be left minding the store, don't you think?" Blake asked.

"Family business," Kai answered.

Now both of Blake's eyebrows went up. "The one who left you here . . . He's your father?"

Kai nodded.

Mr. Blake took a moment and gazed around the store. He stepped over to a rack of T-shirts and thumbed through them. Then moved over to another rack. Then studied some of the transfers displayed on the walls. He looked back at Kai. "None of these items has a price attached to it. How are people suppose to know what it costs?"

That, of course, was the key to his father's scam. The items in the store cost whatever Pat thought the buyer would pay. If you looked like you could pay thirty dollars for a shirt, Pat charged you thirty dollars. But if you looked like you could pay seventy-five dollars, that would be the eventual price once the heat transfers and other "extras" were added on.

Mr. Blake came back to the counter. "Any idea when your father might be coming back?"

"Not a clue," Kai replied.

"When he does, I want you to give him a message," Mr. Blake said. "State law requires that the price of every item be clearly marked on or near that item. Next time I visit this store—and believe me, that's going to be very soon—I expect to see that all the items are in compliance with state law. Can I count on you to relay that message?"

For the first time, Kai smiled. "You bet."

"**D**amn it! Damn it! Damn it!" Pat stomped around the store like a little kid throwing a temper tantrum. Kai had just relayed the message from Mr. Blake that all the items in the store had to have clearly marked prices.

"How the hell am I supposed to make any money?" Pat asked.

"You could sell the T-shirts at normal prices like everyone else," Kai said.

Pat glared at him, and Kai could almost read his mind: Sell a three dollar T-shirt and a seventy-five-cent heat transfer for twenty dollars? Make only sixteen dollars and twenty-five cents profit when he used to make fifty dollars? Was Kai crazy?

"Don't give me any lip, sonny boy," Kai's father snarled.

"Why don't we just pack up and go somewhere else?" Sean asked.

"You want to know why, Mr. Mud-for-Brains?" Pat snapped. "Because yesterday that SOB Buzzy Frankenstein or whatever his name is came in here and made me pay the whole summer's rent in advance. We leave now, I'll lose all that money and it's too late in the season to open a new shop in another place."

"But if we can't make no money," Sean said.

Pat was quiet for a moment. Kai imagined all sorts of bent gears churning around in that sick mind. "We'll make money," he growled. "Believe me, one way or another, we'll make money." He looked at Kai and made a face, as if he'd just bitten into something sour. "So what happened with that Chinese guy?"

"Japanese," Kai said.

"Whatever."

"I gave him a refund."

"You what!?" Pat went to the cash register and pulled it open. He quickly counted out the money inside. The Alien Frog Beast always knew exactly what was in the cash register.

"Two hundred twelve dollars! You son of a bitch! Why'd you do that?"

"I had no choice," Kai said.

"The hell you didn't!" his father shouted. "You tell him you don't know how to work the register. You tell him it's broke. You tell him any goddamn thing you want, but you never give back my money, you hear? You ever do that again, I'll send you packing so fast you won't know what hit you."

Kai was tempted to say that maybe if his father hadn't run away and left his son to fend for himself it wouldn't have happened. But he knew it wouldn't matter. Meanwhile the Alien Frog Beast's face had turned red. He was fuming. "You are nothing but trouble for me, hear that?"

Again Kai was tempted to remind his father that it was he who'd found them a place to stay the night before, when Buzzy had given them half an hour to get out. Meanwhile the Alien Frog Beast pulled out a half-smoked cigarette and lit it. As usual he immediately started to cough. Then, watery eyed and gasping, he gazed around the shop, squinting his eyes. He turned back to Kai. "You're always drawing crap. Why don't you come up with a logo?"

Sixteen

That night while Pat and Sean watched TV in the motel room, Kai pulled a chair out onto the second-floor balcony and sat under the outdoor light. With bugs and moths making kamikaze orbits above him, Kai sat with his notebook in his lap, sketching logos. At first he'd resisted the idea of doing anything for Pat, but then he'd decided what the hell, if Pat wanted him to create a design, he'd create one. Besides, it would give him something to do at night.

In the dark below, someone wandered out into the yard. It was Curtis with a bottle in his hand. He looked up at Kai. "Doin' your home-work, grom?"

"Sort of."

"Then I'll leave ya alone." Curtis pulled out a rusty old beach chair held together with string and tape and sat down with his back to Kai, facing out toward the surfboards scattered around the backyard. Kai sketched for a moment more, then closed his notebook and went down the steps.

"Mind if I join you?" he asked, pulling a folding chair next to Curtis in the dark.

"Only if your homework's done and you're ready for school tomorrow," Curtis joked.

"I think I'm okay on that score," Kai said.

They both looked up at the night sky. The stars twinkled between ghostly drifting cotton ball clouds.

"They're daring me to enter a competition in Fairport in a couple of weeks," Kai said.

"What do you care?" Curtis asked.

"You used to compete," Kai said.

"True. I used to think it was the only thing that counted. The only standard by which a surfer could be judged."

"What changed?" Kai asked. "You didn't just wake up one day and decide it was all garbage."

"That's true too," Curtis said. "It was a gradual enlightenment. You know, grom, judging surf competitions is a pretty subjective business. You're sitting on the beach watching guys who might be a quarter of a mile away perform tricks and throw spray. And all in all it's a fairly small close-knit world. Judges and competitors know each other pretty well. Some like each other, some don't. Sometimes the judges are even competitors themselves. So it can be pretty hard to say just who the best surfer is sometimes."

"You didn't like it because it was subjective?" Kai asked.

"Well, let me put it this way," Curtis said. "Suppose you got two surfers. One of 'em is a real nice guy. Friends with everyone. The other one's kind of abrasive, gets on people's nerves. Now these two boys go out and compete and it's a dead heat. From the beach you really can't tell who was better. Now which one do you think is gonna get more points?"

"You're saying some judges might score one guy higher because they like him more?"

"Damn straight. And I'm not even sure they'd know they were doin' it. If they like one of those boys, it just may appear to them that he's doing a better job. On the other hand, if they don't like one of those boys, they may judge him with a more critical eye. It's just human nature, is all. Although there are other, darker aspects as well."

"Such as?" Kai asked.

"Well, let me caution you that I'm not saying that I know for a fact that anything like this has ever occurred," Curtis said. "But let's just suppose for a moment that you've got this young phenom with a half-million-dollar sponsorship deal with some huge company. Now it is definitely in that company's interest to make sure their boy wins a lot of competitions and gets his name and picture in a lot of surfing magazines."

"So you think the company might bribe some of the judges?" Kai guessed.

"Well, I think that's putting it a bit too harshly," Curtis said. "Could be a nice all-expense paid trip to Tahiti, or maybe just a free lifetime supply of widgets, or whatever that company happens to make. Like I said, I don't actually know of any cases where that happened, but it does seem like a possibility. And that's just part of the answer to the question of why I think I lost interest in the competitive side of surfing. Another part is that big box of trophies under my kitchen counter. See, as a competitive surfer, for a while you're hot and then you're not. New guys come along and they're younger and cooler and crazier and the next thing you know you're getting less ink in the magazines. Now I guess for some people that's enough. To know that they were once on top of that heap. And for other guys like Buzzy, if they can't be on the top of one heap anymore, they just find another heap to climb to the top of."

"I don't care about any of that," Kai said.

"Right," Curtis said. "So you're sitting here feeling like you've got no earthly reason in the world to want to go over to Fairport in a couple of weeks. And yet there's just this thing, this little part of you that wonders why not? That wonders if maybe there's something wrong with you because you don't subscribe to the great American notion that anything and everything can be turned into a competition. That wonders if maybe you are a little scared or uncertain."

Kai gazed up at the stars. What Curtis didn't know was that he'd been ultra-competitive once. He'd dreamed the dream. And paid the worst price imaginable for it.

"The irony is, once you look at competition that way, you'll never be the champ," Curtis said.

"Why not?"

"Because it's just not that important to you anymore. The training, skipping the parties and the girls, taking the crazy risks . . . what's the point? The guys who become the champs really are the ones who just have to win no matter what. You go through all those trophies under my sink, you won't find a single first place. There's some runners-up—times I got real lucky with a move or a wave—and a whole bunch of thirds and fourths. Just enough to score that next plane ticket to Bali or Oahu or wherever. Then when the time came, and I couldn't even get the thirds and fourths, I was prepared and able to walk away."

"Or maybe not taking it seriously is just an excuse for not being good enough to be the champ," Kai said.

"Aw, now look at the psychology major." Curtis chuckled. "Sure, could be just an excuse for not being good enough, or tough enough, or dedicated enough to be champ. But the reason I figure that ain't the case is that I have no regrets. At least, not about that part of my life."

"But you regret not being immortalized like Da Bull," Kai said.

"That's something else. There've been guys who rode bigger waves since Makaha. You ever hear of Ken Bradshaw or Alec Cooke?"

Kai shook his head.

"They both rode bigger," Curtis said, "but hardly anyone remembers them. Now quick, name all the world surfing champions between nineteen eighty and the year two thousand."

"Uh, well, Kelly Slater, Sunny Garcia, Shane Dorian . . ."

"And? What about all the other guys?"

Kai shrugged.

"My point exactly," Curtis said. "Even a world championship doesn't buy immortality. There's something else you need. And whatever it is, that's what I regret not having. But tough luck on me, grom. Now back to your original question. Should you surf in the Fairport competition? Here's my answer: Sure, as long as you're realistic about what you're gonna get out of it. A brief moment of glory, and the admiration of those who you already count as your friends. At best, maybe a tiny step toward something bigger in the world of surf competitions, if that's what you really want."

"What about a chance to open up Screamers to everyone?" Kai asked.

Curtis chuckled again. "I wouldn't hold my breath."

Seventeen

The next morning Kai slept in later than usual. He'd stayed up half the night talking to Curtis, and anyway, the forecast hadn't been very promising, so he didn't think he'd miss much in the way of surfing. He woke up around eight and went through the dunes behind the Driftwood and checked out the waves anyway. As predicted, they were ankle slappers to knee-highs. A month ago the sight of any wave would have been enough to get him stoked, but now it wasn't that exciting, and besides, the short board was practically useless in these conditions. Even Buzzy must've called off the morning's practice session with Lucas, because the only surfers out were Bean and Shauna.

As Kai walked down the beach to wave hello he noticed that there were now more piles of scrap wood. Some were just disorganized heaps. Others were beginning to take the form of bonfires. Bean and Booger's pile in front of Sewers was half heap—half bonfire.

Kai looked out at Bean and Shauna, excited to see that they were surfing Screamers. Part of the reason was that Sewers was unrideable today. But it was still a huge step, since up till now, people who weren't in Lucas's crew were afraid to surf that break even when no one else was around.

Kai went down to the water's edge and watched Bean and Shauna. The waves at Screamers tended to jack up faster and steeper than the mushburgers at Sewers, and Shauna was having trouble catching them. But she was definitely getting better at positioning herself for the wave and, when she did catch one, she popped up without going to her knees first. Bean was just fooling around. He'd left his leash on the beach and was trying to do headstands and walking to the nose backward.

Feeling a bit sleep deprived, Kai sat down.

"Mind if I join you?"

Kai looked to his left and found Spazzy

standing there, hopping and blinking and flapping his hands.

"Be my guest."

Spazzy sat down. While he was still making weird movements and tics, they didn't seem as intense as on previous days. For a few moments they sat quietly, watching Shauna and Bean.

"I can't believe they're surfing Screamers," Spazzy finally said.

"For now," said Kai.

"You mean, if Lucas and his friends come, they'll have to go back to Sewers?"

"Probably."

They watched Shauna go for a wave, pearl nose down, and bite it in the suds.

"She just learning?" Spazzy asked.

"Yeah, but she's totally stoked," said Kai.

"That's so cool," Spazzy said. "The other guy's good. I've seen him before. Really knows how to hold a trim line and walk the board. You hardly ever see young guys surf that way anymore."

"You watch a lot of surfers?" Kai asked.

"Every chance I get. Of course, it's better when my sister isn't around."

"She the one who came down to the beach the other day?" Kai asked.

"Yeah. Major pain in the butt."

"The way she was dressed, looked like you were supposed to go somewhere," Kai said.

"Nah, she dresses like that all the time. She's just . . . ah, forget it."

Kai gave him a curious look. Like it was okay if Spazzy didn't want to talk about her. But also okay if he did.

"Well, she's not just my sister. She's my guardian, too. Like, my parents died and she was left in charge."

"They died?" Kai winced.

"Yeah. Nine-eleven."

"The World Trade Center?"

"Flight Seventy-seven. The one people forget about."

"Huh?"

"Crashed into the Pentagon," Spazzy said. "I know it's not really fair to say everyone's forgotten about it. It's just that when you say nine-eleven most people think of the twin towers. Or that plane that went down in Pennsylvania because the passengers fought back. Hardly anyone talks about the plane my parents were on, and the people who were inside the Pentagon. Altogether there were over two hundred."

Kai nodded slowly. What he didn't say was that the numbers didn't matter. It could have been one person who died. But if that one person was your mother or father, or anyone who was a big part of your life, it was a huge loss all the same.

"Wasn't your sister a little young to become your guardian back then?" Kai asked.

"The whole guardian deal didn't take effect until she turned eighteen," Spazzy said. "Before that my aunt was in charge, but my sister's like one of these people who's been forty years old since the day she was born, you know? Like super-responsible and all that garbage. Actually, it's a major pain."

"How come?"

"She's way too protective," Spazzy said. "It's like she won't let me go anywhere or do anything."

"She's afraid you'll get hurt?"

"That's what she says, but sometimes I think she's more afraid of how people will react," Spazzy said. "Like they won't understand or they'll be scared, or they'll say something mean to me. Sometimes I think she's more freaked about the whole Tourette's thing than I am, and I'm the one with the problem."

Out at Screamers, Shauna finally caught a wave and turned the board down the line. She wobbled for a moment and windmilled her arms as if she was about to lose her balance, but then straightened up and had a nice little ride in the pocket. She had the funniest expression on her face. Like she couldn't believe she was actually doing it. The wave closed out, and Shauna launched herself off the deck into a backward somersault and splashed into the water. Then she jumped up with her arms raised into triumphant fists and let out a whoop.

Kai couldn't help smiling.

"Want to know a secret?" Spazzy said.

"Okay."

"I surf." Something about admitting that made Spazzy get a little hyped up. He started blinking, then twitched and licked the back of his hand and sniffed it.

"Serious?" Kai asked.

"For sure. Been doing it for three years. See, at this school I go to the whole point is to encourage us to try everything we want. So I wanted to surf and Santa Barbara's got some pretty good point breaks. You go about fifteen miles south and you're at Rincon. So a lot of people around Santa Barbara surf and there's this one teacher, Mrs. Lantz, she took me out and taught me."

"You could surf that?" Kai pointed out at the knee-highs now rolling into Screamers.

"Aw, come on, that's tiny," Spazzy scoffed. "This one place we usually go, Campus Point? You get bigger waves than that almost every day. And in the winter it can get major. I mean, eight, ten feet."

Kai looked at him. "You surf in eight, ten feet?"

Spazzy grinned. "No. I'm just saying it's not that uncommon out there."

"Short board or long board?" Kai asked, testing him.

"I got a six-four Channel Islands tri-fin for good days and a eight-six Water Hog for all the rest," Spazzy said. "Al Merrick lives right there in Santa Barbara. That's where his factory is. There's a whole store with nothing but his boards."

"Sweet," Kai said. "So how come you're not surfing here?"

"With my sister around?" Spazzy said. "Get real, dude. She doesn't know anything about it. When we're out in California, she's up at Stanford most of the time going to college. But out here forget it. She's watching me twenty-four-seven. You saw her the other day. She freaks if I even go near the water."

"So where're your boards?" Kai asked.

"Back in Santa Barbara in Mrs. Lantz's garage."

"That's a bummer."

"Not really. I could always buy a board here and hide it somewhere. That's not the problem."

"The problem's your sister?" Kai asked.

"That's part of it," Spazzy said. "But even she can't watch me all the time."

"Then what's the rest of the problem?" Kai asked.

"Mrs. Lantz and I have one rule," Spazzy said. "She'll let me ride anything I think I can catch. But the deal is, someone's gotta be out there with me."

Shauna had climbed back on her board and was riding in on her stomach. She reached the shallows, tucked the board under her arm, and started running toward them, shouting, "Did you see it? Did you?"

Kai nodded. "Way to go, champ."

Without stopping, Shauna dropped the

board on the sand and threw her wet arms around Kai's neck. "I did it! I rode sideways! I had a real ride! Oh, it was so cool! Like how the board slips around and you have to hold the edge. Oh, I can't believe it!" She pulled her head back, looked Kai right in the eyes, and kissed him hard on the lips.

Eighteen

At T-licious, Kai spent the day putting price tags on T-shirts and heat transfers. Pat looked pale and sickly, as if the idea of selling garments at anything less than total rip-off prices made him ill. Kai knew things were really bad when a shapely woman came in and tried on a shirt in the changing room, and Pat didn't even bother to go into the back and watch on the hidden video camera.

Kai took dinner early and walked down to L. Balter & Son, the only funeral home in Sun Haven. Outside the two-story brick building Bean was moving the yellow traffic cones that said FUNERAL TODAY off the street. He was wearing a black suit, white shirt, and black tie.

His long black braid was tucked under the collar of the shirt.

"Have a nice day?" Kai asked.

Bean smirked. "Oh, yeah. Driving dead bodies around always puts a smile on my face."

"Someone's gotta do it," Kai said.

"That's what my old man always says. Along with, 'There's lots of green in black.'"

"Like green as in money and black as in funeral homes?" Kai guessed.

"You got it. Another one of his favorites is that it's steady work," Bean said.

"As long as people keep dying?"

"Right. Burying loved ones isn't the kind of thing families want to do themselves. So what's up?"

"You gonna be around later?" Kai asked.

"Sure. You want to come by?"

"Where?"

Bean pointed at the second floor of the funeral home. Kai looked up and saw green curtains on the windows.

"You live *in* the funeral home?" Kai asked in disbelief.

"Hey, dude, it's free and it's my own place," Bean said. "It sure beats living at home or paying rent."

Kai could have pointed out that it might have been free, but that it also meant spending each night in a building that contained dead people. But he had a feeling Bean already knew that.

"Catch you later," Kai said, and went back to T-licious.

It was close to 11 P.M. before Kai got back to the funeral home. He went around to the back and passed several hearses, including Bean's. Kai pressed the doorbell. From inside came the sound of footsteps coming down a staircase, then the clicking of locks being undone, and the door swung open. Bean stood in the doorway wearing a long black-and-white-checked robe. His long black hair hung loose over his shoulders. He blinked as if for a moment he couldn't figure out why Kai was there. Then he seemed to remember. "Hey, dude."

"If this isn't a good time," Kai said.

"It's cool," said Bean. "Come on up." He turned and headed up the stairs. Kai followed, noticing that the walls of the stairwell were covered with old movie posters. One or two had to do with surfing, but most did not. They reached a small landing with a door. Rather than go straight in, Bean knocked. "Hey, Pauline, we got company. You decent?"

The door opened and Shauna's cousin Pauline stood there clad in a man's long-sleeved white oxford shirt. Kai had a feeling it was the same shirt Bean had been wearing earlier that evening.

"Oh, hi." Pauline smiled and blushed slightly.

"Visiting Shauna again?" Kai asked as he and Bean went into the apartment. The scent of freshly burnt incense hung in the air.

Pauline bit her lip and glanced at Bean, who cleared his throat. "Actually, Shauna doesn't know Pauline's in town. And neither do Shauna's parents, if you get my drift."

"Gotcha," Kai said, and looked around. Bean's apartment appeared to be two rooms. The room they were in had a small kitchenette in one corner, a couch, and some comfortable-looking chairs facing a small entertainment center in another corner, and a desk with a computer in another. Covering the walls were movie, surf, and music posters. On guitar stands were an acoustic and an electric guitar. An amp stood against the wall. Some shelves in the entertainment center were filled with CDs. All in all not a bad crib, considering the rent, and as long as you didn't think about the down-stairs neighbors.

Pauline yawned and covered her mouth with her hand. "I'm wasted, guys. Hope you don't mind if I go to bed."

"No problem," said Bean.

Pauline gave Kai a wave. "Nice to see you again, even though I'm not really here."

Kai waved back. Pauline went through a door into what Kai assumed was the bedroom.

"Think I could go online?" Kai asked.

"Sure," Bean said. "I'll get you going."

Bean logged on and then let Kai sit at his desk. He went over to one of the chairs near the entertainment center.

"Feel like some music?" Bean asked.

"Sure."

Bean put on a CD, the volume low in def-erence to Pauline in the next room. The music was instantly familiar to Kai. Retro rock from a long time ago. He'd heard snippets of it here and there all his life, but had never really paid attention.

"Who is it?" he asked.

"Pink Floyd," Bean said. "*Dark Side of the Moon.* One of the all-time greats."

"Kind of old though," Kai said.

"Nineteen seventy-three," Bean said. "But believe me, worth listening to."

"I believe you," Kai said.

Bean sat down in one of the chairs and started to read *Surfer*. At the computer Kai typed in the URL for Ethan's Web site. It loaded fast, and the photos of surfers, kayakers, hikers, snorkelers, waterfalls, Mt. Kawaikini, Polihale Beach, and the Kilauea Lighthouse mostly looked new or at least recently updated. So it was safe to assume that his mom's old boyfriend, Ethan, was still there.

Kai logged off and got up from the computer. "Thanks, dude."

Bean looked up from his chair. "Finished already?"

"Yeah, just had to check something," Kai said. "I'll get going."

"Don't feel like you have to," Bean said.

Kai jerked his head toward the bedroom. "You've got company."

Bean glanced at the bedroom door, then nodded. "Catch you tomorrow."

Kai went down the stairs and let himself out. Sun Haven was quiet now. The dark air was warm and moist and still. Since it portrayed itself as a family resort town, there were hardly any bars or other sorts of places where people could hang out late at night. Clearly the city fathers wanted it that way, and that was why they were putting pressure on Curtis to shut down the Driftwood Motel, which attracted an "undesirable" crowd. In the case of Sun Haven, "undesirable" meant anyone who wasn't willing to eat in expensive restaurants and shop in expensive stores.

Even on Kauai, Kai could remember people complaining about the big new resorts and condo complexes being built. Thinking of Kauai made him think of his mom and Ethan and the life they'd had there. He wondered if he would ever go back. The thought made him feel lonely. Without actually planning it, he found himself standing across the street from Tuck's Hardware. Jade's apartment was on the second floor. The light was on behind the curtain and Kai saw her silhouette pass twice. It was late, but he didn't feel the least bit sleepy, nor did he want to go back to the Driftwood and share that small room with Sean and the snoring Alien Frog Beast Chief Hockaloogie.

Suddenly Jade's curtain rose and she stood

at the window wearing a plain white oversize T-shirt. Her head snapped up when she saw him. Then she smiled, pulled up the window and leaned on the window sill.

"Can't sleep?" she asked.

Kai shook his head.

"Me, neither," she said. "It's funny how some people can sleep no matter what, while others have the hardest time. As if they're haunted by ghosts who won't let them rest."

"I know what you mean," Kai said.

"Want to come up?" Jade asked.

Kai crossed the street.

Nineteen

The waves picked up overnight, and there was a nice early morning offshore breeze. Kai went down to the beach at sunrise. Buzzy and Lucas were already there. Kai paddled out through the shoulder-high surf.

"So what about Fairport?" Lucas asked when Kai got there.

"What about it?" Kai said.

"You gonna show us what you've got or just pretend to be a soul surfer forever?"

"Come on, Lucas," Buzzy said. "Forget him. Let's focus on work."

Lucas gave Kai a knowing look—as if he'd already decided that Kai would be too chicken to compete—and then paddled over to his father. *Work,* Kai thought. *Buzzy thinks surfing is work.*

Since they were all on short boards, they collected around the same spot near the jetty where the swells started to break. Once again Kai let waves pass for Buzzy and Lucas instead of trying to catch every good one that came in. He still managed to get his share of waves.

The rest of Lucas's crew began to show up. As usual Runt and Sam gave Kai some serious stink eye. Everett nodded. The new guy, Derek, didn't even look in his direction.

Down on the beach, Booger, Bean, and Shauna arrived and waved at Kai. Bean and Shauna paused to zip up their wet suits and wax their boards. Booger slipped on his fins, jumped in the water, and started out through the waves. Kai looked back to see if any sets were coming. Nothing real promising at that moment. He turned and looked back toward shore. Booger was still kicking out. Only he wasn't headed toward Sewers. He was headed toward Screamers.

Like deer going still, Kai could almost feel the sense of alertness flow through Lucas's crew. Even Buzzy grew quiet.

"What's he doing?" Runt asked. No one

answered. It was obvious what Booger was doing.

"Man, I knew it," Sam grumbled. "I just fricken knew it."

Lucas's whole crew was now watching Booger kick toward them. At the same time, they were shooting looks at Kai from the corners of their eyes as if waiting to see what he'd do. Kai had to fight the desire to smile. *Good for you, Booger,* he thought. He hadn't thought the kid had it in him.

"This isn't happening," Sam grumbled. "No fricken spongehead is movin' in on this break. Everett, you know what to do."

It seemed to Kai that Sam said this loud enough for Lucas to hear, as if he was really asking Lucas what he thought. Lucas didn't say a word, as if his answer was, it was up to Sam.

Kai also knew what Sam was planning because they'd once done it to him. They'd wait until Booger caught a wave. Everett would drop in on him to try to ruin his ride, but also to distract him. Meanwhile Sam would be on the next wave. While Booger was busy dealing with Everett, Sam would run him down.

Everett turned and gave Kai a questioning

look. Kai shook his head slowly. This meant war and they all knew Kai was willing to fight.

Booger got out past the break and clung to his bodyboard, his eyes darting this way and that, looking at everything and everyone except the waves. Kai could see he was freaking. He winked at the kid to try to let him know things were okay and he was proud of him for making such a gutsy move, but Lucas's crew was vibing Booger bad. If vibes had been sounds, the air would have been a black roar.

A set was coming in. Booger looked around, trying to assess whether any of Lucas's crew was going to take the first wave. Usually the better surfers let the first wave in a set pass, knowing bigger waves often followed. Kai had a feeling Booger knew this and would try to take the first wave because he thought no one else would. That's exactly what the kid did, spinning his bodyboard around at the last second and kicking with all his might to get into the pocket.

Kai gave Everett a steady look. The guy didn't budge. As if this was one firefight he wasn't going to take sides in. Sam saw that too. Strangely, the kid named Derek didn't move either, but just watched the whole thing silently.

"Crap." Sam started to paddle into position to catch the next wave. It was obvious that with or without Everett, he was going to run Booger down. Sam was so busy paddling for the wave that he didn't see Kai paddling around behind him. The wave started to crest and Sam dug and kicked hard for it. Kai slipped into the water and grabbed Sam's leash.

Twenty

The leash went tight in Kai's hand. For a split second it felt like it was going to pull right through his fingers. Then it went slack, and Kai knew Sam wasn't running over anyone on that ride.

When the leash went tight, Sam was yanked off his board. At the same time, his momentum pulled Kai forward. They were both in the impact zone now, being flung around under the surface, although given the size of the waves that day, it wasn't like either of them had to worry about being seriously trashed. Kai was more worried about his new board banging into Sam's. He got to the surface just in time to see Sam grab the new thruster and turn it upside down.

In a flash Kai knew what Sam planned to do. It was one of the oldest moves in the book. The easiest way to stop a surfer from surfing was to snap a fin off the bottom of his board. As Sam reached for the center fin of the thruster, Kai reached down to his own leash and tugged it with all his might.

Kai's intent was to yank the board out of Sam's hands before Sam could snap a fin off. What he didn't expect was the scream that followed. "Ahhhh!" Sam cried, then grabbed his hand. Something red started to seep out between his fingers. Then Kai realized what he'd done.

Lucas and Buzzy helped Sam go in. Everett followed with Sam's board. Kai followed Everett. On the beach Sam cradled his hurt hand with his good one. Blood continued to drip out from between his fingers.

The lifeguards didn't go on duty until 9 A.M., but Buzzy trotted over to the closest lifeguard stand, searched around under it, and trotted back with a bright orange first aid kit. Sam was sitting on the sand by now, and Buzzy kneeled in front of him and opened the kit. He got Sam to let go of the injured hand. Kai and the others saw the bright red gash between the middle and ring finger on Sam's right hand.

Buzzy wrapped the wound with gauze. Then he and Lucas helped Sam to his feet and led him up the beach toward the parking lot. Everett and Runt followed, carrying their surfboards. The first aid kit was left open for Kai to pack up.

By now Shauna, Booger, and Bean had joined the crowd. They asked Kai what had happened and he told them.

"Serves him right for trying to run me down," Booger said.

"I'm not sure Lucas and his friends are gonna see it that way," Kai said, and headed toward the lifeguard stand with the first aid kit. He was on his way back when Runt came down the beach, followed by Everett.

"You fricken cut his finger off," Runt yelled.

Kai looked at Everett, who shook his head. "Looked like it might need a couple of stitches," the dreadlocked kid said.

"But you were trying to cut his finger off," Runt insisted.

"Runt, get a life," Bean said.

"This means war," Runt snarled, then went to get his board. That left only Everett from Lucas's crew. The guy named Derek was still out surfing Screamers as if nothing had happened.

"Do me a favor?" Kai said to Everett. "You know the T-shirt shop where I work? If you're around town later, maybe you'll stop by and let me know how he is?"

"No sweat," Everett said.

Except for Derek, Lucas's entire crew had gone. The sun was shining, the air was warm, and the waves were feathering blue shoulder-high walls. Kai and his friends stood on the beach for a moment, as if not sure what to do.

"Hey, guys." Spazzy came down the beach with a brand-new wet suit in one hand and a brand-new green-and-blue-striped beach towel in the other. Both items still had white sales tags dangling from them.

"Hey, man," Bean said.

Spazzy twitched, then licked the back of his hand and sniffed it. "How come you're not surfing?"

"Sam just had an accident," Bean said.

"Is he okay?" Spazzy asked.

"We think he's gonna be okay," Bean said.

"What happened?"

"I tried to surf Screamers so Sam decided to get me," Booger said. "Only Kai got Sam first."

"I didn't mean to hurt him, just stop him," Kai added.

"He who lives by the sword dies by the sword," Spazzy said.

Once again they stood around as if not sure what to do.

"I know this feels weird," Shauna said. "Like part of me is saying we shouldn't go back out and surf, because someone just got hurt. But another part of me is saying we might as well surf, because there's nothing else we can do."

"I like that part better," said Booger.

"I guess we could go visit Sam in the emergency room," Spazzy said.

"I'm sure he'd love that." Bean chuckled.

Booger picked up his bodyboard. "Well, I don't know about you guys, but Screamers is wide open and those waves look too good. I'm going back out."

"Hard to argue with that," Bean said. He picked up his board and followed, leaving Shauna and Kai with Spazzy.

"I got a wet suit," Spazzy said. "So I can show you, okay? You'll come out with me, right?"

Kai wasn't certain how to answer. He was always in favor of people surfing, but this seemed like a lot of responsibility, and he was already responsible for one person getting hurt today. "What if something happens?"

"Nothing's going to happen," Spazzy said. "I told you, I've been surfing in California for three years. Nothing ever happened there and it's not gonna happen here. It's just that I made Mrs. Lantz a promise."

Kai looked at the wet suit and the towel and the labels hanging from them. Spazzy had bought them just to show Kai he could surf.

"What are you gonna do for a board?" Kai asked.

Twitching and blinking, Spazzy turned to Shauna. "Think I could use yours for a minute?"

Shauna frowned. "It's not my board. It's Kai's."

Spazzy turned to Kai. "Then we can do it?" It was more of a statement than a question.

"You sure you can surf?" Shauna asked.

"Been surfing for years," Spazzy said. "I swear."

Shauna gave Kai a "so-what's-the-problem?" look.

Kai sighed. He knew he wasn't going to win this debate. "All right, let's go."

Twenty-one

Spazzy tugged his shirt off, then wrapped the beach towel around his waist and started to pull at his shorts. Only, in true Spazzy fashion, the towel didn't stay tucked in and started to slip down his waist. Shauna covered her eyes with her hand and turned away. With his shorts down around his ankles, Spazzy tried to grab the towel and hold it up before it fell to the sand and left him bare-butt naked on the beach. In the process he lost his balance and fell. Now he couldn't get up without letting go of the towel.

"Hold on to that towel, dude." Kai reached down, slipped his hands under Spazzy's arms from behind and helped him up while Spazzy clung to the towel.

"Tell you what," Kai said. "I'll hold the towel from behind and you pull on the wet suit."

It took a while, but they managed to help Spazzy get the wet suit on. "Good thing this is a shorty," Spazzy said. "Out in California I have to wear a full suit. Sometimes it takes half an hour just to get it on."

One thing that amazed Kai about Spazzy was how open and honest he was about his "condition." Kai watched nervously as Spazzy bent down and picked up old #43. He started to feel a little better when the guy pulled the leash up and balanced the board in the middle with the bottom facing inward and the deck facing out. So, at least, it *seemed* like Spazzy knew what he was doing.

About ten feet from the water's edge, Spazzy broke into a run, splashed into the shallows and launched himself and the board into the waves. Kai felt himself relax even more. It looked like Spazzy really had been doing this for years. Kai got on his board and paddled out behind him. Spazzy headed toward Sewers with his back arched, knees bent, and both feet raised, no doubt a habit he'd developed surfing in the cold California winter waters. The guy's paddling strokes were strong and smooth and from the movements of his arms, Kai knew he was using the S stroke that good swimmers, and surfers, use to get extra thrust.

Usually the first time you paddled out in the morning, especially at a break you'd never surfed before, you tended to take your time. You sat up on the board, caught your breath, had a look around, felt the smaller swells rise and fall beneath you, took a look at how the waves were cresting and breaking, checked the water for unwanted guests such as sharks and jellyfish. So it took Kai by surprise when, before they'd even gotten all the way outside, Spazzy suddenly swung the tip of the long board around, took a couple of easy strokes and was on a wave. It happened so fast that Kai didn't even have time to catch the next wave and follow him. In a flash Spazzy was up and in the pocket. His stance was wide and stiff. Not nearly as relaxed and graceful as Bean's, but with his legs spread like that he could shift his weight forward or back, slowing down or speeding up the board at will.

By the time Kai caught a wave, Spazzy was paddling back. Kai kicked out and paddled with him.

"Nice ride," Kai said.

"Thanks, dude. You can't believe how good it feels."

Actually Kai was pretty sure he could believe it.

They caught some more waves. After a while Shauna stood up on the beach and waved at them.

"Uh, I hate to say this," Kai said to Spazzy, "but it looks like Shauna wants the board back."

You could see the disappointment creep across Spazzy's face. Then he glanced at his wristwatch. "I better get going anyway before the Wicked Witch notices I'm gone and sends out the hounds. This was really great, dude. Thanks."

"My pleasure."

Spazzy started to look for a wave to catch in. "Hey, one other thing?" he said. "Think I could leave my wet suit and towel with you? If I take 'em home, I'm gonna catch hell."

"No sweat," Kai said. "Leave 'em on the beach. I'll take care of them."

"Be back tomorrow, okay?" Spazzy said.

"Definitely," said Kai.

Spazzy caught the next wave in. On the

beach he handed the board back to Shauna. Meanwhile, Kai paddled out to Screamers, where Bean and Booger were having a blast in the shoulder-high surf.

"Amazing about Spazzy, huh?" Bean said when Kai got there.

"Yeah, the kid can actually surf," Kai said.

"That's not what I meant," Bean said.

Kai frowned.

"Didn't you notice?" Bean asked.

"Notice what?"

"The second he started surfing, it all stopped. The twitching and shaking. All that nutty stuff just went away."

"You think it was all an act?" Kai asked.

"No way, man," Bean said. "That Tourette's stuff is for real."

"Then I don't get it," Kai said.

Bean shrugged. "I don't get it either, dude. Guess it's just the magic of surfing."

Twenty-two

Later Kai said good-bye to his friends and carried his board and Spazzy's wet suit and towel down the beach and through the dunes to the Driftwood Motel. It was time to change, shower, and grab some breakfast before reporting to work. But as Kai entered the backyard, he came upon a bizarre sight. Two men in blue jeans and black T-shirts with SUN HAVEN FD printed on them were using fire axes to chop Curtis's old surfboards in half, then throwing the broken pieces into the back of a small dump truck. Meanwhile Curtis sat in a beach chair watching, with a bottle of JD in his lap.

Kai's first inclination was to shout at the

men to stop, but the way Curtis just sat there watching gave him pause. What the hell was going on? He started toward Curtis. Before he got there, one of the firemen carried a board over to Curtis and let him inspect it. Now Kai noticed that lying on the ground behind Curtis was a small pile of boards that he had apparently decided were worth saving.

Curtis gave the thumb's down to the board the fireman showed him. The fireman laid it on the ground and swung the axe. *Crack!* The fiberglass broke in half with a sound like a gun shot. Kai grimaced at the thought of it. They were destroying surfboards. This was insane. *Thunk! Thunk!* Both halves of the board got tossed into the back of the truck.

Kai reached the chair. Curtis looked up at him with red-rimmed eyes. It was hard to tell whether they were red from drinking or from tears. He reached into his shirt pocket and pulled out a new pink citation.

"Town tells me these here surfboards are an environmental hazard," Curtis said. "They were to burn up, all this hydrogen cyanide'll get into the air. Know what they say hydrogen cyanide's used for? Gas chambers, grom. That's what they use to kill the killers who've killed.

You ever look at a surfboard and think, 'Death sentence'? Strange world we live in. Strange world." Curtis swept his arm around the yard. "Think of it, grom, all these here surfboards catch on fire, I could turn this whole town into one big gas chamber. Know what the irony of it is? This here's the death of Sun Haven. You're seein' it before your very eyes. These boards go. This motel goes. I go. And so goes the soul of this town. Suffocating under the weight of greed. Pretty soon there won't be anyone left except the rich folks. Everyone else'll have to move inland, where land is still cheap and the ocean is just a faraway distant dream."

Crack! One of the firemen broke another board in two. The sound made Kai wince. "How could surfboards catch fire out here?"

"You never heard of lightning, grom? Stuff's everywhere. Why I bet every year there are thousands of surfboard fires caused by lightning right here in Sun Haven alone. Don't tell me you've never noticed all them charred surfboard remains lying around."

"What about all the surfboards in Sun Haven Surf?" Kai asked. "Wouldn't they be a fire hazard too?"

"No way," Curtis said. "That Buzzy's a clever fella. He's got hisself a sprinkler system." Curtis reached over the side of the chair and picked up a rusty old lawn sprinkler. "I tried to tell these fellas I had a sprinkler system too, but they didn't believe me."

Curtis tossed the rusty lawn sprinkler back on the lawn. One of the firemen came over with the white-and-blue Trigger Brothers board Kai had discovered the first time he'd come to the motel. The fireman held it up in front of Curtis. Curtis glanced at Kai.

"You gotta keep it," Kai said.

"Looks like the grom wants me to save that one," Curtis said. The fireman nodded and added the Trigger Brothers to the pile beside Curtis's chair.

Crack! The other fireman brought his axe down on an old aqua blue Wave Riding Vehicle. Kai didn't understand how Curtis could just sit there and watch. Unless it was like attending a funeral. But Kai had already attended one too many funerals in his life. He didn't need to see this.

Then he had an idea.

"Catch you later, old man," he said.

"If I'm still around," Curtis replied ominously.

Kai carried his board up to the room on the second floor. Pat and Sean had already left for the store. Kai knew he was going to be late for work, but that was too bad. He left the board in the room and went back down the outside stairs. *Crack!* The firemen were still destroying the old boards. Curtis was still sitting in the beach chair watching. The scene made Kai sick. He headed out to the street and over toward Teddy's house.

Twenty-three

Teddy was in the workshop, bent over a gorgeous seven-foot tri-fin, brushing on a gloss coat. Normally Kai knew better than to bother her when she was doing such delicate work, but this was an emergency.

"There's a problem," he said.

Teddy gave him an odd gaze—half puzzled, half warning him not to bother her. She looked back down at the board and continued to work.

"I don't mean to interrupt you," Kai said.

"Then don't," Teddy replied without looking up.

"Right now two guys from the fire department are in Curtis's backyard hacking up his surfboards with fire axes."

Teddy straightened up and stared at him, but Kai had a feeling she wasn't really seeing him. In her mind she must have been picturing the scene. It was strangely easy to imagine. The axes swinging down. The boards lurching and shuddering as if they were in their last death throes.

And then Teddy did something Kai did not expect. She smiled.

And started to apply the gloss coat again.

"You really don't care?" Kai asked.

"About that son of a bitch?" Teddy shook her head as she continued to work. "Not for an instant."

"Look, I don't know what happened between you two all those years ago," Kai said. "But he needs help."

"Not from me he doesn't." Teddy sighted down the surface of the board to make sure the gloss coat was going on evenly.

"He loses that motel, he'll have nothing," Kai said. "It's all he's got. Without it he'll just drink himself into oblivion."

"Is that a promise?" Teddy asked.

"I am serious, damn it," Kai said.

Teddy rested the brush on her workbench. "Why? What do you care?"

"I care . . . because to me he represents the way surfing should be. It's about sharing. It's about being friendly. It's about a common love for the ocean."

"Ah . . . the good old aloha spirit." Her words stank of sarcasm and bitterness.

"That's right."

"Tell you what, Kai. Maybe someday, if you can catch that SOB when he isn't drunk, you should ask him where that aloha spirit was when the best young woman surfer ever to come out of these parts wanted to compete against the men and he wouldn't allow it."

"Why didn't you just go to other surfing competitions?" Kai asked.

"Because when it came to women surfers back then, the competitions were few and far between. I didn't have the means to travel down to the mid-Atlantic states. And forget about Florida. That might as well have been on the other side of the world. But if I could have competed here, maybe I would have gotten a mention in a magazine, or a local sponsor— anything that might have helped me get going. But that son of a bitch wouldn't even let me take the first step."

"Did you ever ask him why?" Kai asked.

"About a thousand times," Teddy said, and started brushing on the gloss coat again.

"What'd he say?" Kai asked.

"Why don't you go ask him?"

"Okay, I will. But you know what's going to happen in the meantime? He's gonna lose everything he has. You know they broke into his shed and took his best boards. Now they're gonna destroy all the rest. They're just grinding him down into nothing."

"Good . . . *Damn it!*" Teddy put the brush down and sighted down the board again. A tiny drop of resin had collected on the rail. "Now look what you made me do."

Kai waited silently while she fixed the mistake and finished applying the gloss coat. Even though Teddy said nothing and hardly even looked at him, he had a feeling she appreciated being left unbothered while she finished the job.

"Nice," Kai finally said. He knew she was finished when she dipped the brush into a jar of acetone.

Teddy turned to him. "Why are you still here? What do you expect me to do?"

"Curtis says that once he's gone, there'll be no place for surfers to stay. All the breaks around here will just be for rich people who can afford the fancy hotels and expensive restaurants. People like you and me won't be able to surf here anymore."

"And you think saving Curtis's butt will stop that?" Teddy asked.

"At least slow it down," Kai said. "Be honest, Teddy. You know it's not right. That's not the way it's supposed to be."

"Says who?"

"I don't know," Kai said. "Me, I guess."

Teddy put her hands on her hips and gazed at him. "You are a strange one."

The workshop grew quiet. Kai wondered what she was thinking. He thought about what must have been happening at Curtis's. Board after board being destroyed. "Look," he finally said. "You do a lot of work for Buzzy. He's got a lot of say in this town. Couldn't you just speak to him?"

Teddy pointed at the board she'd just finished gloss coating. "Know who this is for?"

"Buzzy?" Kai said.

"That's right. Two thirds of the jobs I get come from Buzzy Frank. Without him, I can't make a living. Why would I do anything to jeopardize that?"

"Because maybe some things are more important than money," Kai said.

Teddy gave him a bittersweet smile. "Correction, my young and very naive friend. Maybe some things *were* more important than money. But that was a long time ago."

"So you really don't care if they destroy all those boards?" Kai asked. "Even though some of them were probably the first boards you ever shaped? Like number forty-three?"

"That piece of junk?" Teddy said.

"A piece of junk that practically saved me from going crazy last month and that right now is being ridden by a girl I know who'll probably never be a competitor but is loving it just the same."

Teddy bristled and her faced reddened. Kai wondered if he'd gone too far. He half expected her to tell him to get the hell out of the workshop and never come back. Then something in her face softened.

"From what I've heard, ninety-nine percent of them are busted, dinged, pieces of crap that weren't worth saving in the first place," she said.

"Maybe to you and me, but not to Curtis," Kai said.

Teddy twisted her lips into an expression Kai couldn't read. "Know what? You are a royal pain in the ass." There was actually something affectionate in the way she said it.

"But you'll see if you can stop them?" Kai asked.

"Maybe," Teddy said. "And maybe it's time you got the hell out of here and stopped distracting me from my work."

"With pleasure." Kai turned to go.

"Wait," Teddy called.

Kai stopped.

"If I do decide to do something, you don't tell a soul, you hear? Not your friends, not Curtis, not a single living soul. Understood?"

Kai forced himself not to smile. "Understood."

Twenty-four

The T-shirt shop had a new look. Fewer shirts hung on the racks, and fewer transfers were displayed on the walls and in the display cases. Instead there were now large hand-lettered signs on the walls that said DON'T SEE WHAT YOU'RE LOOKING FOR? JUST ASK.

When Kai got to the store, his father was talking to a young woman with two little kids in a double stroller. Laid out on the counter were two child-size, light blue T-shirts and two small rainbow transfers.

"We'll make matching rainbow shirts," the Alien Frog Beast was saying. "And the names again?"

"Jake and Jack," the mom said. Kai took a

closer look at the kids in the stroller. They were twin boys.

"Okay." Pat opened the display. Inside were some small plain black-vinyl letters. Pat took a few out and laid them over the shirts to show the mom what they'd look like. The mom pursed her lips with disapproval. Kai knew why. The black letters looked awful on the light blue shirts, especially with the rainbows.

"Do you have letters in any other colors?" the mom asked.

"Let me see what I have in the back," Pat said, and went through the door into the back room. Suddenly Kai realized what was going on. It was the oldest con in the book: bait and switch.

Pat came back with a flat plastic case filled with larger letters in all colors. "Would any of these work for you?"

"Oh, yes, they're much better," the young mother said. "Could you even use a variety so they matched the colors of the rainbow?"

"Of course," Pat replied. "I just have to warn you that these letters are a bit more expensive."

"I understand," said the mother.

Kai doubted she really did.

Pat laid the large colorful letters on the shirts. Then he pretended to frown and rub his jaw thoughtfully. "Gee, now those rainbows look awful small."

"Do you have any larger ones?" the mother asked.

"Hey, Sean," Pat called across the store. "Would you go check in the back and see if there are any more of those big nice rainbows?"

"The deluxe color-bright ones?" Sean asked. "I thought we sold out of those."

"There might be a few left," Kai's father said. "Go check, okay?"

"Oh, I hope you have a few left," the woman said anxiously. It was amazing. Pat had already sold her on the larger rainbows even though she hadn't seen them yet and had no idea of the outrageous price he would ask.

Sean stayed in the back for a long time. Kai could imagine what the young mother was picturing in her head: Sean searching through boxes and boxes for the highly desirable and no doubt very expensive deluxe color-bright rainbows. Pat was truly brilliant in an utterly demented way. If the law stated that he had to put price tags on everything he displayed, the answer was to keep a lot of stuff in the back, where it wasn't displayed. Then he didn't have to put a price tag on it, and he could still charge whatever he wanted.

Finally Sean came out with two rainbow transfers. "Would you believe it? We had two left."

"Oh! That's wonderful!" The mother gasped as if it was a miracle. Kai had no doubt that if he went into the back room, he'd find dozens of rainbow transfers in that size.

Ten minutes later, the young mother left the store with two matching personalized rainbow shirts. By the time Pat added up the colorful letters, deluxe rainbows, new special sparkle treatment and color guard, each shirt cost thirty-nine ninety-five. Before tax.

"Christ on crutches," Pat groaned once the woman was gone. He threw his arms down on the glass display case and laid his head on them as if exhausted. Finally he looked up and glanced around, as if expecting Kai or Sean to ask what was wrong. When neither asked, he took it upon himself to explain anyway. "You see how much work that took? I have to do that on every sale, I'll have a heart attack."

Kai looked at his watch. The entire transaction probably took twenty minutes. The total, including the tax Pat would never pay, came to around eighty-seven dollars. Most people worked a lot harder for a lot less.

Pat fixed on Kai. "You're late again."

"Something came up," Kai said.

"Things have been coming up a lot lately. If I didn't know better, I'd think you had a garden or something." Pat smiled to himself, then turned to Sean. "Get it? A garden? Where things come up?"

Sean frowned and shook his head.

"Aw, for Christ's sake." Pat shook his head wearily and asked Kai, "So'd you ever come up with that logo?"

"I had a few ideas," Kai said.

"Where are they?"

"In my notebook back at the motel."

Pat looked out the window. Outside, sunlight glinted off car windshields. People passed wearing bathing suits, flip flops, and hats and carrying beach chairs, umbrellas, and coolers. It was another hot, bright, clear day and most people were headed for the beach. The store was empty.

"Go get it," Pat said. "I want to see what you've got."

To Kai, any reason to leave the store was a

good one. He left fast, before his father had time to change his mind, and headed down the sidewalk. The sun was a yellow fiery ball in the sky, and Kai wished he had a baseball cap or something. A shiny new black hearse pulled alongside the curb. Bean, wearing a black suit, white shirt, black tie, black hat, and sunglasses, was in the driver's seat. He brought down the window.

"'Sup?" Kai asked.

"Get in," Bean said.

"Why?"

"I gotta show you something."

Kai hesitated and squinted into the windows in the back of the hearse. This wasn't the old one he carried his boards around in. In the back, instead of boards, there was a dark brown casket. "Don't you have someplace to go?"

"So do you," Bean said. "Get in, dude. I mean it."

Twenty-five

Kai went around to the passenger side of the hearse and got in. "Where're we going?"

"Belle Harbor."

Belle Harbor was the next town east of Sun Haven. Where to the west Fairport was mostly middle-class residential houses, and Sun Haven was trying to be an upscale, fancy, family resort town, Belle Harbor was known for being a place where only really rich people lived.

"Why are we going there?" Kai asked.

"I'm going there because I got a stiff to deliver," Bean said, making a screeching illegal U-turn in the middle of Main Street. "You're going there because five minutes ago that was the direction a certain red Jeep was going."

"Being driven by a guy with yellow dreads?" Kai guessed.

"You got it."

They got out of Sun Haven. Main Street became Seaside Drive again. Bean had blues playing on the sound system.

"Who's that?" Kai asked.

"Buddy Guy."

"Sounds good."

"Of course."

Kai glanced into the back of the hearse. The shiny dark brown casket had fancy-looking brass handles. "There really a dead body in there?"

"Indeed," Bean answered.

"How come you're taking it to Belle Harbor?"

"People have this strange way of dying unexpectedly," Bean said. "Sometimes one funeral home has more stiffs than it knows what to do with, while the funeral home in the next town is pretty quiet. So the busy one'll farm a few bodies out. Belle Harbor got busy this week so they asked us if we could dress this guy for them."

"Dress?"

"Drain 'em, embalm 'em, make 'em up, dress 'em up in their Sunday best."

Kai was suddenly glad he hadn't had

much for breakfast. "How'd this one die?"

Bean shrugged. "You got me. All I know is, whenever it gets really hot out, the old ones start dropping like flies. Happens every summer. And Belle Harbor's got plenty of old ones."

"Weird."

"Not really. Just life."

"You mean, death."

"Death is part of life," Bean said. "Only it's one of the parts no one likes to think about."

"So how do you know Goldilocks was going to Belle Harbor?" Kai asked.

"I don't," answered Bean. "But there ain't much after Belle Harbor so I figure it's worth a look. In fact, speak of the devil . . ."

Bean slowed the hearse down. Kai instantly saw why. Up ahead, the red Jeep was pulling out of the parking lot of a big barnlike club called 88s that advertised live music nightly.

"Am I good?" Bean asked. "I mean, am I good or what?"

"You're great," Kai said without enthusiasm.

"What's wrong?" Bean asked. "I thought you'd be totally stoked to find this guy."

"I am, Bean, really. I appreciate this. Only now that we've found him, what are we gonna do?"

"Follow him."

"In a hearse?"

Bean turned to Kai and blinked. "You mean, you think he might notice?"

Kai rolled his eyes toward the hearse's ceiling. "Yeah, Bean, I mean, I think most people tend to notice when a hearse is following them."

Bean started to slow down. "Then I'll back off. We can follow from a couple of cars behind. It's not like we're gonna lose him in traffic around here."

Some cars passed the hearse and then Bean accelerated back up to the speed limit. They could see the red Jeep ahead of them. Just before they got to the town of Belle Harbor, the Jeep turned off down a road lined with tall green hedges. Bean followed. Kai tried to see what was behind the hedges. He caught a glimpse of a tall brick mansion at the end of a white pebble driveway. The mansion was so big that he didn't even have time to count all the chimneys before they'd passed.

Ahead of them, the red Jeep stopped at the entrance to a driveway. Bean pulled the hearse to the side of the road. The driveway was blocked by a tall black iron gate with gold points. Goldilocks leaned out and said something into a small intercom box. A moment later the gate opened and he drove through.

"Now what?" Kai asked, remembering that Pat thought he'd gone back to the motel to get his logo sketches, which should have taken about five minutes.

"We wait," Bean said.

"What if that's where he lives?" Kai said. "We could wait a long time."

"He doesn't live there," Bean said.

"How do you know that?" Kai asked.

"People who live in Belle Harbor get special beach stickers for the town beaches. He doesn't have one on his bumper. Also, he had to talk into the intercom. If he lived there, the gate would have opened automatically. Same technology they use for garage door openers."

Kai gave him a look. "Amateur detective?"

Bean reached to the glove compartment in front of Kai and pulled it open. Inside were half a dozen paperbacks with curling covers and well-worn pages. "Mysteries," Bean said. "When you drive a hearse you spend a lot of time sitting and waiting. So I read."

"Okay, so maybe he doesn't live there," Kai said. "Maybe he's just visiting. Could be a long visit."

"Let's wait a little while and see."

Kai jerked his head toward the casket in the back of the hearse. "What about your passenger?"

"He's not going anywhere," Bean replied.

Ahead of them the black gate swung open and the red Jeep pulled out.

"Short visit," Bean said.

The Jeep made a left and headed back up the road toward them.

"Duck," Bean grunted. He and Kai ducked under the dashboard and waited. The vent from the hearse's air conditioner blew cool air into Kai's face. Bean slowly lifted his head and looked in the rearview mirror. "Let's go." He quickly sat up, turned the hearse around, and headed back up the road. By now the Jeep was at least a quarter mile ahead of them and turning onto the main road into Belle Harbor.

The Jeep made two more stops. One at the hardware store in the town of Belle Harbor, and the next at the service entrance to the Belle Harbor Golf and Tennis Club. While they waited, Kai gazed at the perfect fairways and greens, the pristine white sand traps, and the large, old gray clubhouse with its navy blue awnings, each one embossed with a gold seal. It had been hot and dry for the past few weeks, and some lawns in Sun Haven had begun to turn yellow from lack of water. Kai could only imagine that the water bill for this golf club must have rivaled the entire economy of certain smaller third world countries.

It wasn't long before the red Jeep pulled out of the club's service entrance and headed down another tree-lined road.

"Goldilocks is a busy guy," Bean said as he started to follow him again.

"Listen," Kai said. "I really appreciate your enthusiasm, Bean, but how much longer are we going to follow him while he runs his errands?"

"Let's just see where he goes next," Bean said. "One more stop."

Wherever Goldilocks was going next, he was going there fast. Bean had to keep a heavy foot on the accelerator to stay close behind him and several times the hearse took curves so fast the casket in the back thumped loudly and the handles rattled.

"Your friend back there is getting bounced around pretty good," Kai said.

"We'll straighten him up later," Bean replied, leaning forward in the driver's seat as if to see better, his hands gripping the steering wheel tightly.

The hearse flew around a tree-lined curve and past several white signs with black writing that Kai couldn't make out clearly. The next thing they knew, the pavement ended at a tall silver chain-link fence. The hearse shot through the gate. Bean hit the brakes and the hearse skidded, bounced, and rattled to a stop in a rocky, potholed dirt parking lot. Not far away, a flock of seagulls burst into the air, squawking noisily. A large white and gray blob of guano splattered against the hearse's windshield.

"Crap," Bean muttered.

"Exactly," said Kai. He looked through the windows. They were in some kind of a garbage dump. Small mountains of garbage bags. Piles of old white kitchen appliances. Neat stacks of logs.

Clank! At the sound of metal against metal behind them, both Kai and Bean turned and looked out the back window. The tall chain-link gate had swung closed and Goldilocks was wrapping a chain through the posts to keep it that way.

They'd been made.

Twenty-six

"Uh-oh." Bean swallowed hard and turned to Kai. "What do we do?"

Kai was still watching Goldilocks through the back window. The guy finished wrapping the chain around the gate and started to walk toward the hearse. Kai reached for the door handle. "We get out. You stay on your side of the hearse and keep your hands low where he can't see them. Don't say anything. Just look serious and let me do the talking."

"Jesus, Kai, what if he has a gun or something? What if he's gonna kill us and leave us in the dump?" Bean asked with uncharacteristic nervousness.

"Just be cool," Kai said, and got out.

The sun was blistering. Now that they were inland from the ocean it seemed twenty degrees hotter. The intense rays scalded the top of Kai's head. Every single piece of silver and chrome in the dump glistened and shimmered. The mixed scents of hot rubber and rotting garbage hung in the still air, and heat mirages made everything in the distance ripple. Goldilocks stopped about twenty feet away. He was wearing a white T-shirt tucked into khaki cargo shorts, and a cowry necklace around his neck. Kai didn't see any telltale bulges that often accompanied concealed weapons.

"Why were you following me?" Goldilocks asked.

Kai took his time answering. He didn't want to appear scared. "Friend of mine said you might have something we're interested in."

Goldilocks frowned. "And what might that be?"

"I have to tell you?" Kai said.

Goldilocks narrowed his eyes. "Could be any number of things."

Kai glanced at Bean and frowned, then said, "Maybe we made a mistake. Maybe he's the wrong guy."

"I bet you're right," Bean said. "Definitely

the wrong guy. We should probably just go."

"You're not going anywhere," Goldilocks said. His eyes left Kai and traveled to Bean. "How do I know you guys aren't cops?"

"Sure," Kai said. "You see a lot of cops my age. We're not old enough to drive, so we're the ones who ride bicycles."

Goldilocks nodded at Bean. "He could be a cop. Maybe you're just some trick to get me to drop my guard."

"That's a good one. Never thought of it." Kai shrugged. "Could be, I guess."

The words hung as motionless as the hot air.

"How much money you got?" Goldilocks suddenly asked.

It was amazing, Kai thought. He hated to admit it, but he'd learned a few things from his father. Like how to make someone feel like they just had to buy or sell something.

"Enough," Kai answered. "But we could be cops, remember?"

Goldilocks wasn't amused. "What are you doing driving a hearse?"

"You've heard of *undercover* cops?" Kai said. "My friend here's an *undertaker* cop."

Goldilocks smirked. "What's in the back?"

"Casket," Bean answered.

"And what's in the casket?" asked Goldilocks.

"A stiff, what else?"

"Let's see," said Goldilocks.

"You're kidding me," Kai said.

"You want what I got, first you show me,"
Goldilocks said. "One thing's for damn sure.
No cop's gonna be driving around in a hearse
with a dead body inside."

Kai looked at Bean, who shrugged like it
was no big deal. He went around to the back
of the hearse and swung open the door, then
reached in and undid some straps designed to
keep the casket from slipping around. The floor
in the back of the hearse had rollers which
made it easy to slide the casket partway out.
Kai, Goldilocks, and Bean stood in the hot sun.
Its rays reflected off the dark polished wood of
the casket.

"You sure about this?" Bean asked.

Goldilocks nodded.

Bean reached down and lifted the part of
the casket lid that covered the upper half of the
body. They looked down at a thin old man
with just a fringe of white hair around the sides
of his bald head. Kai could see at once that the
body had been jarred during the drive. The

head was turned to the side, and you could see the line where the makeup job stopped and the gray lifeless flesh began. Bean pulled on a pair of latex gloves, then reached into the casket and repositioned the head. The dead guy's arms were lying at his side. Bean took the right hand and laid it across the body. Then he laid the left hand over the right.

"I thought they got all stiff from rigor mortis," Goldilocks said.

"We massage that out while they're still on the table," Bean said. "Weird thing about rigor mortis is, once it's gone it doesn't come back." He picked up the dead guy's left arm again and swung it like a kid playing jump rope.

"Jesus, man, you'll pull the arm clear off," Goldilocks said.

"Wouldn't be the first time," Bean said. "Not like they're gonna look up his sleeve and see that I broke him off at the elbow." He twisted the hand hard. Kai heard something pop. "There goes the wrist," Bean said.

"Christ." Goldilocks turned away, looking a little green.

Bean turned to Kai. "Guess we can put him back, huh?"

"Yeah."

Bean closed the lid and slid the casket back into the hearse, redid the straps and closed the door.

"So what did you guys want anyway?" Goldilocks asked. "Smoke, roofies, special K, X? What's your pleasure?"

Kai had to think fast. "Shrooms," he said.

Bean gave him a look like he had no idea what Kai was talking about.

Goldilocks grinned. "You guys really are a couple of freaks, aren't you. I can try to get you some, but it's gonna take a while. Why not go for some acid instead?"

"'Cause we like shrooms," Kai said.

"Okay. I'll see what I can do. No promises."

"How long?" Kai asked, knowing that was the expected question.

"Don't know. Might take a week, maybe longer. Where can I find you guys?"

Kai turned to Bean. "Give him your cell number."

Bean shot him a major frown, but Kai gave him a "don't-dick-around" look. Bean gave Goldilocks the number.

"Okay. I'll let you know when I get something." Goldilocks walked back down to the gate and unwrapped the chain. The gate swung open.

Kai and Bean got back into the hearse and drove through. Kai even waved at Goldilocks.

"Shrooms?" Bean sputtered as soon as they were back on the road. "What the hell is that?"

"Mushrooms," Kai said.

"Why mushrooms? I *hate* mushrooms."

"What does it matter?" Kai asked. "We're not buying anything from him. I just had to make sure I didn't say something he might have had on him, because then we would have had to buy it. I tried to think of the one thing I could be reasonably certain he wouldn't have."

"Mushrooms." Bean made a face and stuck out his tongue. "So what are we gonna do when he calls in a week and says he has them?"

"I don't know," Kai said. "We've got time to figure that one out."

They rode for a while without speaking. Then Kai remembered something. "Hey, Bean, did you really break the stiff's wrist?"

"Naw. That's just a noise all dead wrists make if you shake them that way."

Kai glanced nervously at his friend. "Can I ask how you knew that?"

"Hey, you know, you gotta do something to keep it interesting."

Twenty-seven

They dropped off the stiff at the funeral home in Belle Harbor and then drove back to Sun Haven.

"Think you'll be out tomorrow morning?" Bean asked. "Surfline's predicting one to three feet, offshore winds."

"Sounds okay," Kai said. "I better remember to bring Spazzy's wet suit and towel with me."

"That reminds me," Bean said. "There's a book in the glove compartment. The one with the squid on the cover."

Kai took out the book. It was a paperback, old and worn out like the others, but with a label that said it was from the Sun Haven Public

Library. The title was *An Anthropologist on Mars.* Kai almost started to read the title out loud, then caught himself. He wasn't sure how to pronounce anthropologist. He wasn't exactly sure what it was, either.

"What about it?" he asked.

"There's a story inside," Bean said. "I think it's called 'A Surgeon's Life.' Check it out."

Kai turned to the story. He really didn't feel like reading it, but he did notice the words "Tourette's syndrome" in the text. "Just tell me, okay?"

"It's about this surgeon in Canada with Tourette's syndrome," Bean said. "The guy's just like Spazzy. He does all this crazy stuff. Hops around, sniffs people, makes crazy sounds. But the second he puts on a surgical gown and goes into the operating room, it all goes away and he's as steady as a rock. Want to know what else? The guy flies his own airplane. Same thing happens. Soon as he gets in the pilot's seat, he's flawless."

Kai riffled the pages of the book. "You took this out of the library?"

"Yeah."

"You just felt like it?"

"Dude, I had to find out what the story

was. I mean, after you met Spazzy, didn't you become like, totally curious?"

"Not really," Kai admitted. "I just figured, he's got this weird condition, but it's not his fault and he seems to deal with it okay."

"Not me. I hear about something like that, I have to learn everything I can about it."

"Afraid you'll catch it?" Kai asked.

Bean glanced at him while he drove. "You want the whole truth and nothing but? Sure, I wanted to know if I could catch it. I mean, you didn't think of that?"

Kai shook his head.

"Well, the good news is you can't. It's not contagious or anything like that," Bean said. "The bad news for Spazzy is that there's no cure. There are some medicines that calm you down, but a lot of people don't like them because they make you sleepy."

Kai was quiet, thinking. They were on Seaside Drive, heading back toward Sun Haven. "So what'd you think of Goldilocks?" Kai asked.

"Not my type," Bean said.

"But definitely the type who could get his hands on all sorts of illegal and stolen stuff, don't you think?" Kai asked. "Booger said the trunk of his car was full of stuff."

"If you're asking me if I could picture him selling stolen surfboards, the answer is yes," said Bean. "But just because I think that, doesn't mean he did. You know how the law works. You have to be able to prove it."

"When you first saw him this afternoon back in Sun Haven, where exactly was he?" Kai asked.

"On Main Street."

"Where on Main Street?"

Bean glanced at Kai and frowned. "I don't know. Just on Main Street. Why?"

"It's important, Bean," Kai said.

"Let me think," Bean said. "I guess right in the middle of town."

"He was driving?"

"No, when I first saw him he was just getting into the Jeep."

"And the Jeep was parked on the street?" Kai asked.

"Yeah, why?"

"So he wasn't just driving through Sun Haven when you saw him. He'd been doing something there."

"I guess."

"Right there in the middle of town, by the bank, the Lobster House, Sun Haven Surf —"

"And about twenty other places of business," Bean cut him short. "Look, I know you'd love to find a way to connect Curtis's stolen boards to Buzzy Frank, but that is a *huge* stretch. I mean, we still don't know if Goldilocks even has the boards. Or if he does, how he got them. I hate to say it, but you're starting to sound like one of those conspiracy theory weirdos. The type who sees a plot behind every rock."

"Maybe not every rock," Kai said. "Maybe just behind every stolen surfboard."

Bean shook his head. "Take my advice, dude. Stick to the Screamers Liberation Front. It's got a more concrete feeling to it."

By now they'd reached the outskirts of Sun Haven.

"Should I drop you at the shop?" Bean asked.

Kai almost said yes, then remembered why he'd left the shop in the first place. "Can we go to the Driftwood first? I have to get something."

"No prob."

Bean parked in front of the motel, and Kai

got out and jogged around to the back. Curtis was sitting almost exactly where Kai had left him earlier that morning. The pile of boards he wanted to keep lay beside his chair. About half the remaining boards still leaned against fences, trees, and any other available vertical surface. The curds of foam and fiberglass left from the great surfboard massacre covered the yard like a thin coating of snow.

"What happened?" Kai asked.

Curtis didn't appear to hear him. The bottle of Jack Daniel's lay empty on the ground beside the chair.

"Curtis?"

"Huh?" The older man blinked as if he'd just woken from a dream.

"How come they stopped destroying the boards?" Kai asked.

"Don't know," Curtis replied. "Seemed like they were having a fine old time killing surfboards and then one of their cell phones rang and the one fella says to the other, 'That's it. Come on, let's go.' Next thing I know, they toss the axes in the back of the truck with all the broken boards and drive away."

"Like maybe they got called to a fire?" Kai pretended to act dumb.

"No, not like that," Curtis said, eyeing Kai carefully. "More like the person who called said, 'Okay, boys, you've had enough fun. Now come on home.'"

"Strange," Kai said.

"Well, I thought so. Then again, what the hell would I know?" But the way Curtis looked at Kai was as if he suspected something.

Kai felt uncomfortable under the scrutiny. "Well, who cares why? I guess the good news is they're gone, and you've still got half your boards left."

Curtis nodded slowly and then gazed away. Kai figured he didn't feel like talking. He went up to the room and got the sketch book, then went back down and out to the hearse.

"Now to the shop?" Bean asked.

"Yup."

A few minutes later Bean dropped him in front of T-licious. "See you in the morning?"

"Right," Kai said, and got out. He went into T-licious. It was now the middle of a hot, sunny day, and the store was empty. The Alien Frog Beast Chief Hockaloogie was sitting near the cash register, reading a newspaper on the glass counter.

"Did I just see you get out of a hearse?" he asked.

Kai nodded.

Pat glanced at his wristwatch. "It's been two hours since I told you to go get that notebook. What'd you do, go to a funeral?"

"Not exactly," Kai said, placing the notebook on the counter. Pat thumbed through the pages and stopped at a circular design with a *T-L* in the center and the words "Team T-licious" in fancy script forming the perimeter. It was actually the one Kai liked best, and he was surprised his father liked it too.

Pat pressed a nicotine-stained finger down on the sketch. "This one."

"Okay." Kai felt an unexpected sense of pride.

"What do we do next?" Pat asked.

"This is just a sketch," Kai said. "Next I do an actual finished piece of art."

Pat grinned, revealing small, yellowed teeth. "And then we can have our own surf team, right?"

Kai nodded. The way Pat looked at him made him realize something he had not considered before. This wasn't just about doing a logo. This was part of a new scam.

Twenty-eight

The next morning at sunrise, Kai was on the beach waxing up. Despite the early hour the air was already warm. He knew he would be hot in his wet suit today. It was time to get some surfing trunks and a rash guard. He finished waxing and picked up his board. He was just about to head into the water when Lucas and Buzzy came down the beach. Buzzy was wearing a shorty wet suit, and Lucas was in a white long-sleeved rash guard and orange surf trunks.

"How's Sam?" Kai asked. He half expected Lucas to say something nasty like, "What do you care?"

Instead Lucas said, "He's okay. It wasn't that bad. Just a couple of stitches."

"It was an accident, you know," Kai said. "I thought he was gonna snap one of my fins off."

Lucas put his board down and started waxing. "You gonna enter the Fairport competition?"

Kai didn't answer.

"Let me guess," Lucas said. "You'll think about it, right? That's your answer to everything."

Kai knew he was being baited. It would have been easy to take the bait, but he had a better idea. He dropped his voice so Buzzy wouldn't hear. "How about you, Lucas? Did you think about it? Or was it someone else's idea?"

Everybody has a face they wear for the rest of the world. It's the face they want everyone to see and judge them by. Some people would call it an expression, but to Kai it's like a mask. But every once in a while, in a moment of stress or surprise or just relaxed good cheer, they drop the mask and reveal their true face. That's just what Lucas did. He stiffened. Above the collar of the rash guard, his neck began to grow red. Then he picked up his board and headed for the water.

Just as they had on other mornings, Kai,

Lucas, and Buzzy shared the waves at Screamers. By eight o'clock Runt and Everett had arrived. So had Shauna, Booger, and Bean. Still not ready to surf Screamers when there were other surfers to watch out for, Shauna stuck to Sewers. Bean went with her. Mostly, Kai suspected, to keep her company and avoid the crowd.

A little while later Spazzy appeared on the beach carrying a brand-new six-foot-two tri-fin. He stopped by the wet suit and towel Kai had left for him, changed clothes, waxed up his new board, and hit the water.

And started paddling straight out toward Screamers.

"What the hell?" muttered Runt, out in the waves near Kai. But Kai paid him no mind.

Spazzy got outside. Except for Runt, hardly anyone in Lucas's crew vibed him. Kai had a feeling they were starting to accept the fact that Screamers was no longer their private domain. And besides, Spazzy was probably the last person in the world who'd let a little stink eye bother him. After all, when you had Tourette's syndrome, you probably got stink eye every day of your life.

Spazzy got almost all the way outside when a nicely shaped wave suddenly popped up.

Since no one else was going to ride it, he spun around and took off. Kai realized this was probably the first time that summer that the kid had ridden a short board, since the day before he'd been on old #43. But Spazzy had no trouble adjusting to a board that was three feet shorter and considerably less buoyant. He not only popped up and did a nice bottom turn, but managed a snap at the top and then trimmed out down the line.

A few more decent waves came in, but Kai let them pass and waited. Spazzy paddled back out and gave him a big, happy smile.

"You were really starting to rip that last one," Kai said.

Spazzy grinned proudly. "Thanks, man."

Another wave was coming in. Ever eager to ride again, Spazzy started to turn his board, but so did Runt. While Spazzy didn't seem to notice Runt, the red-haired kid had his eyes on Spazzy, as if wondering which of them was going to claim the wave.

"Hey, Spazzy," Kai called.

Spazzy looked up from his board, surprised. Kai jerked his head toward Runt. Spazzy swiveled, saw the other kid, and instantly sat back on his board, giving Runt room to take off. Runt shot Kai a brief, puzzled glance, as if he couldn't understand why Kai had called Spazzy off the wave and didn't know whether to thank him for it. Then he was in the wave and riding.

Meanwhile Spazzy gave Kai a questioning look.

"You just caught a wave and Runt hasn't had one for a while," Kai explained.

"Gotcha," Spazzy said. He understood. You couldn't ask other surfers to share their waves with you unless you were willing to share yours with them.

He and Kai sat in the water, bobbing up and down as the smaller swells rolled by, scanning the horizon for the higher crests that would signify the next good set. As usual Buzzy and Lucas were off by themselves, working on the "moves" Lucas would show at Fairport.

"You know the competition? I'd like to enter too," Spazzy said.

"You serious?" Kai asked.

"Think about it," Spazzy said. "This guy with Tourette's syndrome out there competing. Showing everyone he can surf with the big boys. Think anyone's gonna make fun of me after that?"

"If anyone makes fun of you now, they're just plain stupid," Kai said.

"Yeah, but maybe you can make stupid people smarter." Spazzy nodded at Runt, who was paddling back out after his last ride.

Kai couldn't help but grin.

"Uh-oh," Spazzy suddenly muttered. He turned his board around so that he was facing straight out, as if watching for the next set, his back to the beach. Kai looked at the beach and saw what the problem was. Spazzy's sister was walking toward the water, her head twisting left and right as if she was searching for someone. And she wasn't alone either. A short stocky woman was walking with her.

Kai sat on his board parallel to the shore, so that he could keep an eye on the waves and the beach.

"What're they doing?" Spazzy asked without turning around.

"Looking around the beach," Kai said. "Who's the other lady?"

"Marta," Spazzy said. "Our housekeeper. Has either of them looked out here?"

"Not really."

"Yeah, this is the last place they'd think I'd be," Spazzy said.

Spazzy's sister and Marta stopped at the water's edge, then parted and walked in opposite directions.

"I hate to say this, but your sister looks a little freaked," Kai said.

"What am I supposed to do?" Spazzy asked. "She ever finds out what I'm up to, I'll never get near the beach again."

"Can she really stop you?" Kai asked.

"Easy. All she has to do is take away my board and my credit card."

"But she can't *really* stop you," Kai said. "I mean, you could always borrow a board."

"She could make it really hard," Spazzy said. "Believe me."

Marta and Spazzy's sister were still walking along the beach. Neither of them had yet looked out at the water.

"You really think you could enter the Fairport contest without her knowing?" Kai asked.

Sitting on his board, Spazzy's shoulders slumped. "I don't know."

"Maybe you should just tell her," Kai said.

"She would freak, I mean, totally freak. You have no idea."

"I guess not," Kai said. "But at some point

you have to start living your own life, don't you? I'm not saying it has to be now or even this summer. But how much longer are you gonna wait?" The strange thing was, even as the words came out of his mouth, Kai realized he could have been talking about himself.

It took a while for another set to come in. When it did, everyone was eager to jump on it. Runt took off on the first wave. Lucas nailed the second. With the third looming over them, Spazzy and Kai traded looks. Spazzy nodded and Kai kicked into the wave and slashed down the face, ending with a front side tailslide just before the close out.

He paddled back.

"I have an idea," Spazzy said when Kai got outside again. "Suppose I have everyone over for a Fourth of July pool party? That way she can meet you and see that you're okay. Maybe after that, if I tell her I've been surfing with you guys, she won't freak as bad."

"It's worth a shot," Kai replied.

"Yeah, maybe that's the way to go," Spazzy said.

That was the last they spoke about it. By now Spazzy's sister and housekeeper were both so far away that Spazzy could start catching waves without worrying about being seen.

As usual Kai surfed until a little after 9 A.M., then headed back to the motel to get ready for work. His father was waiting for him at T-licious.

"You finish that logo yet?" he asked.

Kai showed him the finished piece of art.

"Good, good, I like it," Pat said.

He seemed to be in a good mood, which was fortunate considering what Kai had in mind. "I need to take the Fourth of July off."

"You've been taking a lot of time lately," Pat said.

"I work plenty for you, and I should be able to take time when I feel like it."

The Alien Frog Beast thought for a moment. "Sure, go ahead. In fact, you picked the right day. Enjoy yourself."

It was too easy, Kai thought. There was no doubt in his mind that his father was up to something.

Twenty-nine

On the morning of July Fourth Kai and his friends surfed. The waves were small, mostly knee to waist high, and the swell was coming directly out of the south in the form of slow-moving mushburgers. It was one of those mornings when the surfing might actually have been better at Sewers than Screamers. At least, over at Sewers they were definitely getting more rides, and Kai and his buds had no problem moving from Screamers over to their old break.

At one point Kai and Bean were sitting outside, waiting for the next set.

"No work today?" Bean asked.

"Got the day off," answered Kai. "How about you?"

"Same here," Bean said. "We'll just be busier tomorrow. Like my dad always says, 'People can't wait to die.'"

Kai had to think about that for a moment. "That's sick, Bean."

Spazzy paddled over to them. He pointed over at Screamers, where Lucas and his crew were bobbing in the water like corks.

"Why don't they come over here?" Spazzy asked.

"That's an interesting idea," Bean said. "But no way."

"Let's see," Kai said, and waved until he was certain Lucas and the others saw him. They sat on their boards and didn't move or respond.

"They just can't lower themselves," Bean said.

It wasn't long before the onshore winds picked up and blew the weak surf out. Kai and his friends went in and started building the bonfire for that night. Down the beach, opposite Screamers, Lucas and his friends had also come in and were stacking scrap wood into a huge cone-shaped pyre. Sam was there, his right hand bandaged, carrying pieces of wood with his left hand.

By noon the winds died down and the

ocean went flat. Even on the beach the temperature rose to uncomfortable levels. Kai wasn't sure he'd ever seen the sand so crowded or counted so many beach umbrellas. The way people splashed in the shallows reminded him of a crowded swimming pool.

Kai, Booger, Bean, and Spazzy all worked bare chested. Sweat ran down their faces and their skin turned red.

"Anyone want to go to Pete's?" Booger asked, wiping the sweat off his forehead with his hand.

Pete's Hubba Hubba Seaside Saloon was the closest place on the boardwalk that sold sodas. It had a patio with tables shaded by umbrellas. They started up the crowded beach. A lot of people stared at Spazzy and his herky-jerky way of walking. The funny thing was, with the sand so hot, Kai and the others were also hopping and dancing.

"You guys better stop it," Spazzy warned. "Or people are gonna think we're *all* weird."

At Pete's they got sodas and crowded around a table with an umbrella over it. All around them sat people eating Pete's specialties: chilicheese dogs, chilicheese fries, and chilicheese burgers.

"You guys know how to get to my house?" Spazzy asked.

"I'm sure we can find it," Bean said. "It's not like this is a big town or anything."

"Five o'clock, right?" Booger said.

"Yeah."

"Should we bring anything?" Shauna asked.

"Just bathing suits and something dry to wear," Spazzy said.

They finished their sodas. Other people were crowding around Pete's patio with trays of drinks and food, waiting for a table to open.

"Guess we better get going," Bean said.

They got up, threw out their cups, and started across the boardwalk . . . and came face-to-face with Lucas and his crew.

"Impressive stack of wood you got there," Runt said, jerking his head toward the beach. From the boardwalk Lucas's pyre looked at least twice the size of the one Kai and his friends had made.

"Yeah, well, we didn't have one of our fathers buy our wood and have it delivered," Booger shot back. "We went out and found it ourselves."

"Now, now, children," Bean said. "Let's not argue."

"I know what you would say," Lucas said to Kai. "It's not about competing, right?"

Instead of answering, Kai turned to Sam. "How's your hand?"

"What do you care?" Sam asked.

"It was an accident," Kai said. "I thought you were going to snap a fin off my board."

Sam didn't reply. Probably, Kai thought, because he really *had* been planning to snap off one of Kai's fins.

"How long before you can surf again?" Kai asked.

"Go to hell." Sam stepped around Kai and continued toward Pete's. Some of Lucas's crew followed, but Lucas hung back.

"Still thinking about Fairport?" he asked Kai.

Kai nodded.

"Not much to lose by entering," Lucas said. "I mean, we all know how well you can surf." His words seethed with taunting sarcasm.

"We'll see," Kai said. He and his friends started down the beach. About halfway there, Bean stopped and looked back. Kai followed his gaze. Shauna was still on the boardwalk, talking to Deb Hollister, Lucas's girlfriend.

"What do you think that's about?" Bean asked.

"You got me," said Kai.

Thirty

The address Spazzy had given Kai was on the east side of town, a part Kai had only passed with Bean on the way to Belle Harbor. He strolled along Main Street past some stores, restaurants, and a few fancy beachfront motels, then found himself walking along a tall pink concrete wall, too high to see over. At the next corner he made a right down a street leading to the beach and found himself in a community of beautiful modern houses with large windows and pools and tennis courts.

Kai walked to the end of the street and up the driveway of one of the most beautiful houses he'd ever seen. It was large, but not huge or fancy. Instead it was a low, modern, one-story structure nestled in the dunes, with grayish, weather-beaten siding. Parked in the driveway was a black Mercedes Benz station wagon with California license plates. Kai went to the front door and rang the bell.

The housekeeper, Marta, opened the door. She was wearing a black skirt and white blouse that sort of reminded Kai of a waitress's uniform.

"Hi, I'm here for the party," Kai said.

"Please." Marta swept her arm in a gesture for Kai to go in. He stepped into the living room. It was filled with sunlight. The other side of the room, which faced the beach and ocean beyond, was all tall sliding glass doors. There were bright, colorful abstract paintings on the walls and sculptures here and there and sleek modern-looking furniture. Hanging on one wall was the largest flat-screen plasma TV Kai had ever seen.

A woman Kai recognized as Spazzy's sister stood by one of the sliding doors, looking outside where Spazzy and his friends were in the pool. It was a hot, sunny summer day, but Spazzy's sister was wearing navy blue slacks and a light blue polo shirt. When she saw Kai, she came toward him with her hand held out.

"Hi, I'm Jillian Winthrop," she said, shaking his hand in a businesslike manner. "You must be Kai. Caleb has said so much about you."

It took Kai a moment to remember that Caleb was Spazzy's real name. Somehow he had the feeling that Jillian wouldn't appreciate hearing her brother referred to by his nickname.

"I hope it's mostly been good," Kai said.

"Oh, yes, he's . . . he's quite taken with you," Jillian said. The look she gave him felt piercing, protective, and suspicious. As if she was trying to peer inside and make sure that Kai's intentions regarding her brother were good. At the same time suspecting him merely because he wanted to be friendly to a guy who behaved so strangely.

"He's a cool guy," Kai said.

Jillian forced a smile on her face, as if deep down she secretly believed that that could not possibly be true, but was willing to go along with it. In the meantime Kai could see that Spazzy had been right. His sister dressed, acted, and sounded like she was much older, but she was just a few years older than Bean at most.

"Well, I'm sure you'd like to join your friends," Jillian said, guiding him toward the glass doors facing the pool. "It's very nice to meet you."

"You too," Kai said, and stepped outside into the sunlight. At first no one noticed him. Shauna and Spazzy were sitting at the edge of the pool with their feet in the water and their backs toward him. Bean was lying on his back on a big silver raft the size of a mattress, his eyes covered by shades and his long black braid hanging over the edge of the raft and into the water. Booger was swimming under the crystal blue surface with a mask and flippers. On a nearby table under the shade of an umbrella was a large hero sandwich sliced into sections and a big bowl of chips. On the ground beside the table was a cooler filled with ice and sodas. Music was playing on some outdoor speakers.

"Hey, look who's here!" Booger said after popping up for air. Everyone turned and said hello to Kai. Spazzy got up. While he still jerked and ticked a bit, it wasn't nearly as pronounced as it had been the first few times Kai had been with him.

"Glad you could make it," Spazzy said, and pointed at a cabana behind the diving board. "You can go in there and change into your bathing suit."

"No, that's okay," Kai said.

Spazzy blinked very quickly, and his eyebrows formed a puzzled V. "What do you mean? This is a pool party, dude."

"Yeah, well, I spend so much time in the water that it doesn't matter that much to me," Kai said. The truth was he kept meaning to buy some surf trunks, but his father barely gave him enough money to eat, and the ding repairs he did at Teddy's were going toward paying for the custom-shaped thruster she'd given him. Any extra money he got seemed to slip through his fingers for drinks and surf wax.

Spazzy licked the back of his hand, then sniffed it, then licked it again. Kai realized he was deep in thought. He gestured toward the cabana and spoke in a low voice the others wouldn't hear. "There's plenty of trunks inside. And when you're done, make sure you take a pair home with you."

For a moment Kai was tempted to say that he appreciated the offer, but didn't need it. But it wasn't true. That would have been pride talking.

"Thanks, man," he said, and went into the cabana. On the shelves were lots of matching, fluffy blue-and-white-striped towels. Hanging on hooks were a dozen different men's and women's bathing suits. At first Kai couldn't understand why Spazzy and his sister would need so many. Then he realized that the suits were different sizes and were probably meant for guests. Kai found a pair of green-and-blue trunks and pulled them on. Then he grabbed a towel and went back out.

Spazzy was sitting with Shauna on the edge of the pool again. "You hungry?" he asked.

Kai shrugged a little. The truth was he hadn't even been thinking about food until he saw that hero, but now it was looking pretty good.

"Go ahead, have some," Spazzy said. "Just don't fill up. You don't want to spoil your appetite for later."

"What's later?" Kai asked.

"A clambake on the beach."

Kai put a slice of hero and a big handful of chips on a paper plate, grabbed a Coke from the cooler, and joined Spazzy and Shauna at the side of the pool. He let his legs dangle in the pool water. The temperature was perfect. Bean drifted over on the raft. Booger surfaced near them and held on to the edge of the pool. Kai watched as both of them stared

at the scars on his right leg. Neither said anything.

"Water feels great, huh?" Bean said.

Kai nodded and bit into the hero.

"Spazzy can make it any temperature he
wants," said Booger. "It's a heated pool."

"So you could actually use it all year
round?" Shauna asked.

"I guess," Spazzy said. "Only we close the
house just before Labor Day and don't come
back until after Memorial Day."

"You mean, for nine months of the year
nobody uses it?" Bean asked.

Spazzy nodded. "Not while my sister and
I are back in California at school."

"What does Marta do?" Shauna asked.

"She takes care of our house in California,"
Spazzy explained.

"But you just said you and your sister were
at school," Booger said.

"We go home on the weekends sometimes,
and that's where we go for holidays," Spazzy
said. He wasn't bragging. In fact he sounded as
if he almost didn't realize that not everybody
had two homes that were hardly used.

"Is all this, like, since nine-eleven?" Kai
asked.

"Oh, no, my parents always had these houses," Spazzy said.

"What did they do?" Shauna asked.

"Like in business," Bean added in case it wasn't clear.

"They worked for the family business," Spazzy said. "It's a company my great-grandfather started."

"What kind of company?" Bean asked.

Spazzy began to twitch and blink. "You're gonna laugh. You know those plastic screens with the blue or pink stuff at the bottoms of urinals?"

Shauna frowned, but Kai, Bean, and Booger grinned knowingly.

"Serious?" Kai asked.

Spazzy nodded. "The Winthrop line of disposable urinal screens with or without integral deodorant blocks in fresh mint, fruity cherry, or bubblegum."

"Whoa, that's *way* more information than I needed," Bean said. He floated closer, so that the edge of the raft bounced against Shauna's knees. "Don't turn around," he whispered. "Spazzy, your sister's still standing by that window, watching us."

"I told you, she's super overprotective,"

Spazzy said, twitching and ticking again. "This is the first time I've ever had friends over. I mean, like, it's the first time I've *ever* had friends, period. At least around here."

"Does she have any friends?" Bean asked.

"Back at college," Spazzy said.

"So you guys come here for the whole summer and, well, you know," Booger said.

"Like, have no friends?" Spazzy finished the sentence for him. "Basically. But we still have fun. We go to the beach and take drives and we see a lot of movies."

"I thought she didn't like to take you where there were crowds," Kai said.

"We have a system," Spazzy said. "My sister figures out when the cineplex is gonna be the least crowded. We either go in and sit down way before everyone else or we come in at the last second, when it's already dark. It's not that hard."

Shauna leaned forward and spoke in a low voice. "Why don't we ask her to come out and join the party?"

"No way," Spazzy said. "I mean, you can ask, but she'll never do it."

"Why not?" Booger asked.

"She just won't," said Spazzy.

"How old is she?" asked Shauna.

"She just turned twenty."

"That's silly," said Shauna. "She's only two years older than Bean."

"A year and a half," Bean said. "I turned eighteen in January."

"Look, you can ask, but she won't do it," Spazzy said. "You'll see. She's like forty years old trapped inside a twenty-year-old body."

"Help! I'm trapped in a forty-year-old body," Booger said.

"It's no joke," Spazzy said. "Not when you have to live with her every day."

Thirty-one

After a while Jillian did come out of the house, but only to suggest they shower and change into dry clothes before heading down to the beach for the cookout.

"It sometimes gets a little buggy in the evening," she said. In one hand she held out a spray bottle of Off! and in the other some kind of Cutter bug stick. "I brought out both of these, in case some of you prefer the spray while others like the rub-on type."

She left them on the table and took the tray with the rest of the hero sandwich inside. The ice cooler had wheels and Marta wheeled it in.

"Two kinds of bug spray?" Booger said. "She really is like forty."

"Told you so," said Spazzy.

They showered in the cabana and changed clothes.

"So when are we gonna light the bonfire?" Booger asked once they were ready to head down to the beach.

"I guess after dinner when it gets dark," Bean said. "Spazzy, you think your sister will let you come down to the fire?"

"It's doubtful," Spazzy said.

"What if we invite her, too?" asked Shauna.

"That's even more doubtful," said Spazzy.

From the pool area they followed a wooden walkway over the dunes and out to the beach. Because this part of Sun Haven was mostly residential and didn't have motels or resorts, the beach here had fewer people on it. Halfway to the water there was yet another surprise awaiting them. A balding man with a gray ponytail, and wearing a white apron, was cooking lobster, chicken, and hot dogs on a grill. Once again there was a cooler with drinks, bowls of chips, plastic plates, knives, and forks.

"Do you guys, like, ever cook for yourselves?" asked Booger.

Spazzy's faced flushed slightly. "Not much. I mean, Marta does most of the cooking."

"You're rich, aren't you?" Booger said.

"I don't know," Spazzy said. "I never asked."

"But you could have anything you want, right?" said Booger.

"Hey, Boogs, chill," Bean said. "That's like private stuff. Maybe the dude doesn't want to talk about it."

"I don't care," said Spazzy. "I mean, I guess you're right. I can get whatever I want, but all I ever want is music and surfing magazines and videos, and maybe a couple of wet suits and boards. There's nothing else."

A kid wearing a black helmet and goggles shot past on an ATV, glancing briefly at the cookout before continuing down the shoreline.

"How about an ATV?" Booger asked.

"Are you kidding?" Spazzy said. "My sister would never let me."

"Dinner's ready," said the man with the ponytail.

Spazzy let the others go first. The ponytailed man offered everyone half a lobster or chicken. Kai hesitated.

"Take the lobster," Spazzy said.

"I've never had it," Kai said.

Shauna looked up. "You've never eaten lobster?"

Kai shook his head.

"That's amazing," Shauna said. "I practically grew up on the stuff."

"Yeah, but your father was a lobsterman," Bean said.

"Take the lobster, Kai," Shauna said. "I'll show you how to eat it."

Kai took the lobster, a baked potato, and a small dish of melted butter. When the ponytailed man handed him some folded white plastic, a small metal fork with thin tines, and something that looked like a nutcracker, Kai gave Shauna a look. She nodded for him to take those things too. They sat down together in the sand.

"Okay, first the lobster bib," Shauna said, unfolding the plastic. It was a thin white bib with a picture of a red lobster on it, and reminded Kai of the bibs people put on infants at mealtime. She tied the ends around her neck so that the bib hung down in front of her. "This is so you don't get lobster juice all over your clothes."

Kai didn't put it on right away. "Somehow I manage to eat a lot of things without getting food on me."

"Not lobster," Shauna said. "Just put it on, okay?"

Kai unfolded the bib and put it on.

"Now, in my family, we always start with the claw." Shauna picked up the lobster's body in one hand, took the lobster's claw arm in the other and twisted it off. Then she clamped the nutcracker around the claw and squeezed. When the claw broke, juice sprayed against her bib.

"See?" she said. Using the thin fork, she dug out the succulent white lobster meat inside.

Kai followed her example and dipped a chunk of claw meat in melted butter, then ate it. It was delicious.

"Pretty good, huh?" Shauna asked.

"I could get used to this," Kai said.

"I bet."

While she showed him how to get the meat out of the lobster's arms, Kai asked, "What were you and Deb Hollister talking about today?"

"Nothing."

"Yeah, right."

"Is everything okay?"

They looked up. Jillian had come down to the beach. Even though it was still an hour before sunset and pretty warm out, she'd knotted a white sweater over her shoulders.

"It's great," said Shauna. "Thanks so much."
Everyone nodded in appreciation.

"Oh, it's nothing," Jillian said.

A slightly awkward silence followed. "Well, have fun," Spazzy's sister said, and started back up the beach.

"Why don't you join us?" Bean suddenly asked.

Jillian stopped. "Oh, I couldn't."

"Sure you could," Bean said. "I mean, have you had dinner yet?"

"Well, not really."

"Then let me fix you a plate." Bean was on his feet getting her a plate of food before Spazzy's sister could protest. But even with a plate of food in her hand, Jillian looked uncomfortable. Kai was pretty sure she couldn't see herself sitting on the sand. Bean seemed to sense that, too.

"Over here," he said, and led her toward a large gray driftwood log lying in the sand a dozen yards away. Jillian followed and soon they were sitting together on the log, eating and talking. Kai couldn't help thinking that for a tall, nerdy, long-boarding undertaker-in-training with a Fu Manchu mustache and a black braid that reached down to the middle of his back, Bean was definitely in control when it came to the opposite sex.

Shauna leaned toward Kai. "He really has a way with the ladies."

More than you could imagine, Kai thought, remembering the secret trips to Sun Haven that Shauna's cousin Pauline had been making. "I guess looks aren't everything."

"No." Shauna gazed dreamily at Kai. "But they sure don't hurt."

Over on the log Jillian laughed out loud. Spazzy actually lifted his head and blinked, not from a tic, but from astonishment.

"Was that my sister?" he whispered.

"Must've been," Shauna said.

"Wow," Spazzy said. "I can't remember the last time I heard her laugh. I mean, except in a movie theater."

They sat on the beach eating lobster, corn on the cob, and baked potatoes. The thin strips of clouds had vanished, and the sky was a vast, flawless blue. It was unusual for the wind to remain calm all afternoon on such a hot day, but as a result the ocean was as glassy as the surface of Spazzy's pool, broken only by a pod of fish splashing on the surface as they chased bait.

The sun was just starting to set, but the beach was far from empty. It had been a hot day and people seemed reluctant to leave. Had there been fewer beachgoers, Kai might have noticed the trouble that was approaching them.

Thirty-two

"**A**w, cute. Look, it's a cookout."

Without even looking up, Kai knew it was Sam. Runt, Everett, Derek, Lucas, and a couple of girls including Lucas's girlfriend, Deb Hollister, were also there. Kai was struck by the realization of who was driving the ATV that had passed them earlier. He should have known it was Runt.

Kai and his friends stood up. Spazzy was twitching like crazy, and some of the girls with Deb Hollister stared at him with horrified expressions on their faces.

"Cute bibs," Runt taunted.

Meanwhile Derek went over to the grill where the man with the ponytail was cooking.

With his bare hand, the tattooed, pierced guy picked up a chicken leg and thigh right off the hot grill and took a bite.

"Excuse me," Jillian said. "That's not for you."

Derek chewed on the chicken and looked at her with an almost blank expression. Kai couldn't figure out whether there was a lot going on inside the guy's head. Or nothing. Both possibilities were kind of unnerving.

"Don't you guys have anything better to do than crash our parties?" Booger asked. "Why don't you have some parties of your own?"

"We have plenty of parties," Runt shot back. "We just make sure you don't know about them."

"Then, why don't you pretend you don't know about this one?" Spazzy said.

Runt glanced over at Lucas as if awaiting orders.

"I guess I'm just thinking about your philosophy of sharing," Lucas said to Kai. "You want us to share our waves with you. How come you don't share your parties with us?"

"Maybe I would have," Kai said. "But this isn't my party—it's Spazzy's."

It was a dumb mistake and Kai knew it the second it left his lips. He forgot to call Spazzy by his real name. Kai glanced at Jillian, who was suddenly wearing a massive frown.

"It's okay," Spazzy said to his sister. "It's just what everyone calls me. I don't even care. I mean, I'm so used to it, I don't even notice anymore."

But between Derek taking the chicken and Kai calling Spazzy by his nickname, it was clear that Jillian had had enough. She took Spazzy aside to speak to him in private, but Kai and the others could hear every word she said.

"What's going on here?" Jillian asked her brother.

"Nothing, really, they're just some guys we know," Spazzy said.

"How?" Jillian asked.

"Just from hanging around," Spazzy said.

For a moment Spazzy's sister was silent, but Kai could see that her brother's answer was not going down well. Jillian turned to Lucas. "You're Lucas Frank. I've seen your picture in the local paper. You're a surfer."

"That's right," Lucas said.

Jillian studied Lucas's crew. "You're all surfers?"

Sam, Everett, and the others nodded. Jillian turned to Kai. "And you and your friends?"

Kai nodded. He could almost see Jillian putting it together in her head. All these kids were surfers. How in the world could her brother know them? Where would he have met them? Spazzy's sister turned to Lucas again. "This is a private gathering. I would appreciate it if you would leave my brother and his friends alone."

Lucas glanced at his crew and jerked his head, then started down the beach. The crew followed, except for Derek, who went over to the grill and picked up a cob of corn for the walk home.

When Lucas and his friends had gone, Jillian stared for a moment at Spazzy. Then she turned and walked back toward the house.

Thirty-three

Up to that point Spazzy had been in a really good mood, but now he grew quiet. They finished the cookout talking about movies and TV and music. Everything, it seemed, except surfing. The sun was starting to go down, and they began to hear the pops and cracks of fireworks.

"Time pretty soon for the bonfire," Bean said.

An awkward silence passed.

"Hey, Spazzy," Kai said. "Maybe you could get Jillian to come?"

Spazzy twitched, licked the back of his hand, and sniffed it. Stuck a finger in his ear. Blinked. Shook his head. "Thanks, Kai, but it's not happening. When I go back in the house, it's gonna be the fricken Spanish Inquisition."

"The what?" Booger asked.

"I'll explain it to you later," said Bean, then got up. "We still have to thank her for the party."

With Bean in the lead, they walked up the beach, across the walkway over the dunes, and around the swimming pool. Through the sliding glass doors they could see Jillian inside, sitting on a couch, reading a book. Spazzy slid open the door closest to her. She looked up with an expression that was just a few degrees warmer than icy. A mask.

"Everyone wants to say thanks," Spazzy said.

Jillian nodded.

One by one, Kai and his friends told Spazzy's sister how much they appreciated the party.

"You know, if you'd like to come down to the bonfire," Bean said.

"Thank you, Larry," said Jillian.

"It's Bean, really. It's been a long time since anyone called me Larry."

"Bean," Jillian said flatly.

"And everyone calls me Booger," said

Booger. "I mean, it doesn't have anything to do with my nose or nothing. It's because I bodyboard."

Jillian nodded, but said nothing. It was pretty clear that she understood they were saying that they all had nicknames. The others backed out through the sliding door, but Kai stayed a moment longer. He put his arm around Spazzy's shoulder. "I just want you to know that we think your brother's a cool guy. It doesn't matter what syndrome or nickname he has. He's always welcome to do stuff with us."

Jillian nodded again.

"And you, too."

Jillian blinked. As if hanging out with a bunch of scruffy local surf rats was something she'd ever do.

Kai rubbed Spazzy's head. "Catch you later, dude. And thanks again."

With the sky turning blue-gray, Kai, Shauna, Booger, and Bean went back over the dunes and started down the beach, preferring to walk back along the water. While Kai had been inside with Spazzy and Jillian, Bean had been explaining the Spanish Inquisition to Booger.

"She's not really gonna torture her own brother, is she?" Booger asked.

"Of course not," said Bean, "but one way or another she's gonna find out that he's been surfing without telling her. And that's probably just as bad, because for Spazzy, not surfing is gonna be torture."

"What a you-know-what," said Booger.

"Wait," said Shauna. "She threw that whole party for him. She can't be that bad."

"I don't think she's bad at all," said Bean. "She just feels super-responsible."

"She's got to let the guy live," said Kai.

"See, that's the key to the problem," Bean said.

"What do you mean?" Shauna asked.

"It's the Fourth of July," Bean said. "The whole world is out at parties and sitting around bonfires and watching fireworks. What's she doing?"

"Reading a book," said Booger.

"Exactly. So sure, we all know she's got to let Spazzy live," said Bean. "But first someone has to show *her* how to get a life."

They passed half a dozen bonfires and dozens of groups of people sitting on the beach, watching the fires and fireworks. In the distance one fire burned more brightly than any other.

"Bet a quarter that's Lucas's fire," Bean said. "Any takers?"

No one took him up on the bet. Fireworks were going off constantly now, like small arms fire in some war, with larger artillery shells now and then tossed in. The sky crackled and glittered with bottle rockets and roman candles. The red-hot embers rising above the bonfires added to the show.

By the time they reached Screamers, Lucas's bonfire rose up in front of them like a flaming volcano. There were probably three dozen people around the fire, enjoying a full-blown party. Kai spied Buzzy filling a red plastic cup from a keg. Near him Dave McAllister handed out rockets and cherry bombs from a suitcase stuffed with fireworks.

"I didn't think fireworks were legal in this state," Kai said as they passed behind the fire and the party.

"They're not," Bean said. "Except when you're Buzzy Frank and it's the Fourth of July."

Bang! A loud explosion went off a few feet from them. Kai and everyone else jumped.

"You think someone threw it at us?" Booger asked once they'd calmed down.

"Maybe," said Kai. "But it could have been an accident."

They stopped at Bean's pyre, still dark and unlit. Bean kneeled in the sand and took a box of matches out of his pocket. "Let us all now pray to Kahuna, the great god of surf. That he may provide us with big beautiful swells, steady offshore breezes, freedom from harm or surf-related injury, and peace among all surfers."

He reached into the pile of wood and pulled out a plastic bottle of isopropyl rubbing alcohol. Fires near the water were often hard to start because of the dampness, but newspaper, twigs, and an old rag drenched in alcohol usually did the trick. Bean poured out the alcohol and lit a match. Ignited by rags and newspapers at the base of the pile, the fire began inside the stack of wood.

Bean backed away and sat with Kai, Booger, and Shauna on the sand, expecting to watch the fire grow inside the pile of wood and eventually envelope it.

Ka-boom!

Thirty-four

Kai remembered the flash of bright white light inside the pile of wood, and the explosion— probably the loudest sound to ever strike his ears. He remembered being knocked backward to the sand, and the sharp clatter of wood falling onto wood. And then, through the ringing in his ears, he heard the sound of laughter. He opened his eyes and saw the silhouettes of a crowd backlit by Lucas's bonfire. They were the ones who were laughing. Still trembling with surprise, Kai looked around to make sure Bean, Booger, and Shauna were okay. Like him, they were all in the process of pushing themselves up from the sand. They looked stunned and wide eyed, but okay. After the explosion the pile of wood had collapsed in on itself, snuffing out the fire.

Even though Kai wanted to get up right away, he stayed down for a few moments, gathering his thoughts and waiting for the shaking to stop. By now he knew what had happened. Someone had stuck something inside the pile of wood. He rose to his feet. Bean and Booger were also starting to stand. Shauna was still sitting, her knees pulled under her chin, her hands over her face. She was crying.

Kai reached down and placed his hand on her shoulder. "Come on, let's go." He helped her up. She was also trembling from the shock and surprise.

"Probably two or three M-eighties bundled together," Bean was saying.

"Someone could've gotten hurt," said Booger, his voice shaky.

"They probably figured the wood would contain most of the blast," Bean said.

Shauna was on her feet now, sniffing and quivering, but not really crying anymore.

"You okay?" Kai asked her.

She nodded.

Kai led her toward Bean in a way that meant he wanted him to take her. Then Kai started toward the crowd at Lucas's fire.

Most of them had laughed at first, but had now gone quiet. Not because Kai was approaching them, but because they'd seen the shocked looks on Bean's and Booger's faces, and heard Shauna's sobs.

Buzzy Frank stepped out of the crowd to face him. Kai stopped. He could feel the pulse in his forehead pounding. The sudden burst of adrenaline from the blast was still throbbing through his veins.

"It was a joke," Buzzy Frank said with a forced grin.

"It wasn't funny," said Kai.

"Hey, welcome to Sun Haven." Buzzy Frank actually extended his hand as if to shake.

Kai stared at the man's hand and then at the man himself. "I said, it wasn't funny."

The grin left Buzzy's face. Kai waited for him to say something, but Lucas's father was silent.

Finally Kai turned and walked away.

He caught up to the others on the boardwalk. Bean had left the hearse in the parking lot. By the time Kai reached Bean's car, Shauna, Booger, and Bean were all inside. Kai leaned into the passenger-seat window, where Shauna was sitting.

"You okay?"

"Yes, thanks. It just caught me by surprise," she said.

"Join the club," Kai said.

"What'd Buzzy say?" Booger asked.

"That it was just a joke," Kai answered.

Bean snorted. "Some joke. So, you want a ride back to the Driftwood?"

"No, thanks, I'll walk," Kai said. "Catch you guys in the morning?"

"If my ears ever stop ringing," Bean said.

Kai tapped the roof of the hearse and backed away. His friends waved as Bean pulled out and drove into the night.

Kai walked back to the beach. The bonfires were quietly burning now, and the barrage of fireworks had slowed. A lot of people were leaving the beach, and he recognized Everett and Jade walking toward him.

Kai stopped.

"Hey." Everett shoved his hands into his pockets and stared down at the sand. Jade crossed her arms in front of her.

"Dude, I'm sorry about that," Everett said.

"Me too," said Jade.

"It's not like it was your fault," Kai said.

"Still," Jade said.

"It was incredibly stupid," said Everett.

Bang! A firecracker went off a dozen yards away. It was far enough that it didn't catch any of them by surprise. But just the same, it was a reminder.

"Well, see you around." Everett headed up the beach. Jade remained behind with Kai.

"Haven't seen much of you lately," she said.

"Been busy," Kai said. "Nothing personal."

"It's not that girl who was with you tonight, is it?" Jade asked.

Kai shook his head.

"I see her around you a lot."

"I sort of taught her a little about surfing and lent her my board."

"Then you must like her," Jade said.

"She's a good kid."

Jade raised an eyebrow. "And what am I?"

"Superfine," Kai said.

"Does that mean we're leaving the beach together?"

It was incredibly tempting, but Kai shook his head. "I'd like to, but I can't. Not tonight."

Jade stepped close and pressed her lips near his ear. His nose filled with the scent of her perfume. "Don't make me wait too long," she whispered, then nipped him on the earlobe.

Thirty-five

Kai walked along the back edge of the beach where it started to rise toward the dunes. Ahead in the moonlight he saw someone coming slowly up the beach from the water, limping slightly. It was Curtis wearing a pair of dripping trunks with a towel draped over his shoulder. His wet salt-and-pepper hair was plastered down on his head. Kai stopped near the walkway and waited for him.

"That you, grom?" Curtis asked in the dark.

"I thought you weren't supposed to swim at night because of sharks," Kai said.

"About the only sharks you ever see around here are sand sharks," Curtis replied. "Hell, I've probably got more teeth than they do. Besides, any shark takes a bite out of me, he's liable to be given a breathalyzer test."

"Last I knew, sharks don't breathe," Kai pointed out.

"Then a gill-a-lyzer test, or whatever the hell it is they do." Curtis looked back at the ocean. "You have a good Fourth?"

"Pretty good." Kai considered telling Curtis what Buzzy had done, then decided against it. It wasn't as if he'd be telling Curtis anything about Lucas's father that he didn't already know.

"Nice night, huh?" the older man said.

Kai looked at the dark water. It was as flat and smooth as he'd ever seen it, the twinkle of the stars reflecting individually off the surface, the moonlight forming a glittering highway to the horizon.

"Guess there won't be much surf for the next few days," Kai said.

"Au contraire, grom. Tomorrow morning it'll be perfect. A little small for my tastes, but you and your friends will like it."

Kai looked again at the flatness of the water, the total lack of a breeze. "I think you've had too much to drink, old man."

"You'll see," Curtis said.

They followed the path through the dunes

to the back of the Driftwood. Instead of going into the motel, Curtis wrapped the towel around his shoulders and sat down in one of the beat-up beach chairs. He turned it so he was looking up at the moon. "Got time for a beer, grom?"

Thanks to the adrenaline still racing through him, Kai wasn't at all sleepy. "Sure."

"Should be a couple in the fridge."

Kai went around to the office and through the back door into Curtis's apartment. As usual the place was a mess. Kai could smell the slightly rotted scent of garbage before he set foot in the kitchen. The sink was filled with dirty dishes, the counter covered with empty frozen pizza and chicken pot pie boxes. Kai opened the refrigerator, found two Coronas, and headed back outside.

"Here you go," he said, handing one of the bottles to Curtis and sitting down gently in an ancient beach chair.

"Thanks, grom." Curtis took a pull on the bottle. "Always take time to look at the moon. No matter where you are. Gives you a sense of perspective."

"How's that?" Kai asked.

"They say that son of a bitch is four point

six billion years old. How old are you, grom?"

"Fifteen," Kai said.

"Like I said, kind of puts things in perspective," Curtis said.

"What perspective's that?"

"How the hell do I know?" Curtis grumbled. "It just does, is all. Damn, you ask too many questions, grom. Can't you see it interferes with me trying to play the role of the wise old surfing curmudgeon?"

"Was it different being a professional surfer back when you did it?" Kai asked.

"Oh, yeah," Curtis said. "Nothing like it is today. There was no prize money to speak of. Mostly it was sponsorships and photo shoots for magazines. If you figured in the hours we spent traveling and lugging our crap around, we would have been better off working in some factory making minimum wage."

"But you weren't doing it for money," Kai said.

"That's for damn sure. It was the adventure, the women, the glory, and an intense distaste for any kind of life that involved wearing a tie, punching a clock, and having a boss."

"So you wish you hadn't stopped?" Kai asked.

"Hell, yes, but my body got worn out. How long you think you can go partying all the time, drinking, not sleeping, then spending days in the water getting smashed onto reefs, then getting on airplanes, eatin' all kinds of crappy food, and doin' it all over again? Sooner or later your body says, 'The hell with this, boss, give me a break.' Of course, you can't stop. Can't skip the next contest. Because then you won't be in the magazines the next month and your sponsor'll be all over your sorry butt, asking what the hell they're paying for if you're not in the magazines where all the groms and grems and poseurs can see you. So you keep going and you get ground down in the rankings, and these new young hotshots come up, and they've got fresh bodies and fresh stoke and they haven't been dragged across too many reefs yet. Haven't bit it hard at Pipe or got a leash wrapped around some coral head and nearly drowned."

"How do you stop?" Kai asked.

"Usually with a prolonged stay in a hospital," Curtis said. "Multiple fractures, staph infection, food poisoning, or just plain exhaustion. Take your pick."

"And that's it, huh?" Kai said.

"Hell, no. No one gives up the glory and the babes that fast. You take the time to heal and rest up. You stop partying and start exercising and eat right. You get that maturity, that 'old-man-of-the-tour' crap. But now you got new problems you never had before. First, being sensible and mature ain't sexy, and it don't sell shoes and sunglasses, so you start to lose your sponsors. And second, now you got something you never had before—pure, unadulterated, uncompromising fear."

"Of getting hurt again?"

"Of everything, grom. Of getting hurt again, of getting knocked so low in the rankings you don't get invited to the big events, of losing the girls to the new hotshots, of being ignored by the magazines. Basically you've learned something you didn't know before— that the party don't go on forever, and the day's coming when you won't get invited anymore."

"But what you're really saying is the competition's not so bad," Kai said.

"No, it's not so bad," Curtis said. "In fact, it's a lot of fun. You just gotta understand its limitations. It ain't the magic bullet. It might change your life for a little while, but unless you're a fricken six-time world champion like Kelly Slater, it ain't gonna change it forever." Curtis swiveled his head and looked at Kai. "You still trying to make up your mind about that Fairport contest?"

Kai nodded. "Lucas has pretty much dared me to enter."

"That alone's a good reason not to, if you ask me," Curtis said.

"Except that it could shut him up once and for all," Kai said.

Curtis shrugged. "Then do it."

Thirty-six

The next morning at seven forty-five Kai stood on the second-floor balcony of the Driftwood Motel and stared at the waves in amazement. Curtis's prediction had come true. The sets were only medium size, but they were perfect. The sea looked like blue-green corduroy, like a photo from a magazine. Kai yawned. On any other morning he would have gone back to bed. But not this morning.

He carried Spazzy's wet suit and board over the dunes. It was close to 8 A.M., nearly two hours later than Kai usually got down to the beach. The sun was already well into its daily journey and the air was starting to feel hot. For the first time, he didn't wear a wet suit. Instead he wore the trunks Spazzy had given him and a T-shirt. One way or another he'd try to scrape together the money for a rash guard, but for now that could wait.

Lucas, Buzzy, and Everett were down near the tide mark. Lucas and Buzzy were kneeling over a board while Everett opened a tripod and set a small silver camcorder on it. Buzzy and Lucas briefly glanced in Kai's direction, then back down at Lucas's board. They'd turned it on its deck and were hunched over the fins. Kai kept his distance. He couldn't be certain of what they were doing, but he had a feeling he knew.

It was an old surf competition trick, especially among groms who couldn't really do spectacular moves and had to rely on big spray to wow the judges. You balled surf wax up into little beads and "dimpled" the fins. For some reason only a theoretical physicist could probably explain, it seemed to increase the amount of spray you got during a snap.

As for Everett, it was obvious that he was there to record, not surf. Kai got on his board and paddled out. It felt strangely easy without a wet suit on. The waves were smooth, with just a trace of ripple from a slight easterly breeze. Screamers was going off like perfection. As Kai paddled out and looked up into the cresting waves, he saw a school of medium-size fish outlined in the green water like a painting.

Lucas and Buzzy paddled out. This morning there were no nods. No indication of recognition. With his father coaching, Lucas worked on snaps, trying to get more and bigger spray. After a few rides, they'd go in and review Lucas's rides on the camcorder, then come back out. Kai caught waves at will. It was one of those rare mornings when the waves were ripping, but oddly easy to paddle into and catch at the same time.

After a while Bean showed up and paddled out.

"Hey." Bean's eyes had bags under them, and even out in the water on his surfboard he only appeared half awake.

"How are your ears?" Kai asked.

"What'd you say?" Bean pretended to be deaf for a second. Then he jerked his head at Buzzy and Lucas. "They say anything?"

"Won't even look at me," Kai said.

Bean smirked. Then he closed one eye and squinted at Kai with the other as if he didn't have the energy to use both eyes at the same time. "You look different."

"No wet suit," Kai said. "First time this summer. Bean, did you sleep last night?"

Bean nodded. "Big mistake."

"Huh?"

"Went to bed around five thirty. Bad idea. If you're only going to get two hours' sleep, sometimes it's better not to get any at all."

"What were you doing until five thirty?" Kai asked.

"Just talking." Before Kai could ask who'd he'd been talking to, Bean gestured at Everett on the beach with the tripod and camcorder. "We going to be in a movie?"

"I think it's for Lucas and Buzzy," Kai said.

"Whoa, serious preparation for Fairport." Bean yawned. "Time to wake up." A set was coming in and he spun his board around and paddled into it.

An hour of nearly nonstop surfing followed, before they once again found themselves floating together outside, waiting for waves.

"Unbelievable day!" Bean grinned.

"You awake now?" Kai asked.

Bean shook his head. "With surfing this good? No way, I must be dreaming."

By nine thirty Kai had been in the water

for only an hour and a half, but already had more rides than he often got in an entire morning. If every morning of his life could begin like this, things would be pretty good. He was so satisfied he *almost* didn't mind going to work. Truth be told, if he'd had a real, honest job, he might not have minded at all.

Bean went in with him.

"You sure you've had enough?" Kai asked.

"Strange, huh?" Bean said. "Some days you're out there in crap waves for six hours, just trying to put together a couple of good rides. Then you get a day like today with so many good rides so fast, you feel completely satisfied in an hour or two." He covered his mouth with his hand and yawned. "Besides, I think I want to go back to sleep."

They stopped by Everett and his camcorder.

"S'up?" Kai asked.

"Looks great out there," Everett said.

"Yeah, how come you're doing this?" Bean asked.

"Two reasons," Everett said. "First, this is what I'm into. Second, I'm being paid."

"No way," Bean said.

"Buzzy wants Lucas to see what he's doing

and how he can improve, and I'm only too glad to oblige."

"Well, I hope you get to catch a few waves before it blows out," Kai said.

"Thanks, dude," Everett said. "I'll try."

Bean and Kai continued up the beach. They stopped by Spazzy's untouched wet suit and board, and gazed sadly down at them the way soldiers might look at the rifle of a wounded comrade.

"He would have loved it this morning," Bean said.

"Yeah," said Kai. "It's too bad about his sister."

"Hey," Bean said, "you never know."

Thirty-seven

That perfect day came and left, and the ocean went flat after that. Each morning Kai stood on the balcony, searching the liquid horizon for the darker-colored bands of sets, but saw nothing. The few weak waves that did manage to come in broke on the shore. So in the mornings Kai helped Teddy build boards. Gradually she was letting him do more and more work. Now, in addition to the rough planing, she was letting him do some of the laminating and glassing.

Kai spent the rest of each day and evening at T-licious, where Pat was still running the "Don't see what you're looking for? Just ask" scam.

"You look at the sketches I did?" Kai asked his father one afternoon when the store was empty.

The Alien Frog Beast looked up from his newspaper. "Not yet. I'll let you know." He started to look back down, then raised his head as if he'd just remembered something. "Don't make no plans for tomorrow. I'm gonna need you all day while Sean's gone."

"Where's he going?" Kai asked.

"Don't matter," said Pat.

This was definitely strange. Kai wished he didn't care what his father was up to, but it was impossible to ignore, especially since any new scam could have an unwanted effect on his life. So later, when Pat went out, Kai asked Sean what was going on.

"I don't know," Sean said.

"You taking the truck?" Kai asked.

"Yeah. Back to that same place in Brooklyn you and I went to. I guess he figures I don't need you with me because I been there before."

"So you're picking up some stuff?" Kai asked.

Sean nodded. "A lot of stuff."

This was weird for two reasons. First, there

were still lots of shirts and sweatshirts on the racks in the store, and the back room was filled with boxes that had yet to be opened. Why in the world would his father be getting more merchandise now? And second, the Alien Frog Beast would never let Sean take the truck anywhere alone. Not unless something was going on that he really didn't want Kai to know about.

That evening Kai received his customary five dollars for dinner and walked over to Pete's Hubba Hubba for a chilicheese dog and fries. He'd just sat down at a table outside when Bean pulled up in the hearse. Bean got out and headed straight for Kai. "Guess who called?"

"Goldilocks?"

"You got it."

"What'd he say?" Kai asked.

"Wants me to call him back."

Kai patted the bench beside him. "Have a seat."

Bean sat. "I don't like this, Kai. I really don't. This guy could do a reverse lookup on the Internet, get my name and address."

"I didn't think they could do reverse lookups on cell phone numbers," Kai said.

"If he wants that info, I bet there are ways."

"Then he's probably thinking the same thing," Kai said. "We could get his name and address."

"Yeah, but we're not going to do anything," Bean said.

"We know that, but he doesn't," Kai said. "Why don't we call him and see what's up?"

"What if he's got the mushrooms?" Bean asked.

"Let's just call him and see," Kai said. "When you get him on the phone, tell him I'm here too."

Bean took out his cell phone and held it toward Kai. "I have an even better idea. Why don't *you* call him?"

"It's better if you do," Kai said.

"Why?"

"Because then he can't put you on the spot," Kai said. "If he asks a tough question, you say, 'Wait a minute. I have to ask my friend.'"

"Ah . . ." Bean nodded and smiled slightly. "Gotcha." He dialed the cell phone and held it to his ear. "Hey. Yeah, one of the guys you met at the garbage dump. Uh-huh. Yeah. Oh.

Well . . . Okay, hold on, let me tell my friend."
Bean turned to Kai. "He couldn't get the
mushrooms, but he says he can get pharma-
ceutical mescaline."

Kai pretended to think about it. "No, I
don't think so." At the same time he motioned
to Bean not to hang up.

"Sorry, I guess we're not interested," Bean
said. "Yeah, it's cool. Uh, so . . ." He frowned at
Kai, not knowing what to say next.

"Hey," Kai said as if he just had an idea. He
purposefully spoke loud enough so that
Goldilocks could hear over the phone.
"Remember in the garbage dump he said he
could get all kinds of stuff? Like what did he
mean?"

Bean listened to the answer. "Uh-huh, uh-
huh. Okay, hold on." He turned to Kai.
"Electronics, sports equipment, stuff like that."

"Not surfboards," Kai said.

Bean pressed the phone to his ear. "Oh,
really? No way." He gave Kai a thumbs-up
sign. "Hold on. I'll tell him." He turned to Kai.
"He's got some really good used boards, but
they're practically collector's items, so they're
not cheap."

"I was looking for something cheap," Kai

said. "I don't know. Maybe we should look at them anyway. What do you think?"

Bean pressed the phone to his ear. "You hear him? Tonight?" He looked at Kai, who shook his head. "Can't do it, tonight."

"Can we just give him a call when we can do it?" Kai asked.

Bean kept the phone to his ear. "Yeah. We'll call you. Cool. Yeah. You hear about any shrooms, you give us a call, okay? Cool." He snapped the cell phone closed, then pretended to slap his head. "Shrooms. I can't believe it."

"Isn't it amazing?" Kai asked. "I mean, what do you know? He's got a bunch of good used boards. Almost collectibles."

"Yeah." Bean smirked. "Incredible coincidence. So we tell the cops, right? I mean, that's a no-brainer."

Kai straightened up. Bean's expression quickly changed to one of anguish. "No, Kai, don't shake your head. Don't do this to me. We found the guy. Now it's time for the police."

Kai didn't move a muscle. He was thinking.

"Listen, dude," Bean said. "I am serious. This guy's into drugs, stolen property, who knows what else. This is *serious* stuff. Let's not mess around. We go to the police, tell them what we know, then back away, and let them take care of it."

All Kai said was, "No."

Thirty-eight

The next day the surf began to pick up, as if somehow it knew that the Fairport contest was only two days away. Sean was gone all day and Kai worked in T-licious. That evening he stopped at Ice Cream after dinner. He no longer had to stand in line. All he had to do was wave through the window at Shauna and wait. Sooner or later she would come out with a vanilla cone covered with Reese's Pieces.

"I don't know why I'm so nice to you," she said as she handed him the cone.

"Neither do I," Kai said.

Shauna let out a deep sigh. "Well, you should know."

"Surf's picking up," Kai said. "Think you'll go out in the morning?"

"If I can find Bean," Shauna said. "My board's in his car. I've been calling all day, but he hasn't picked up."

"That's weird," Kai said. "He's always around."

"I know," Shauna said. "Usually I don't even have to call. I just wait until I see the hearse pass the shop. I didn't see it once today."

"Maybe we should take a walk down to the funeral home," Kai said.

"Sure, I could take my break now. Give me a second, okay?" Shauna went back into the shop to take off her apron.

"Hey, you," someone said.

Kai turned. Jade was standing on the street, wearing a tight, black, low-cut sports top and shorts. Sweat dripped down her forehead. She was wearing running shoes and jogging in place.

"Didn't know you were a runner," Kai said.

"I'm just full of surprises." Her forehead glistened and her cheeks were red. She licked a drop of sweat off her lips and kept bouncing in place. Kai had to concentrate to keep his eyes from wandering. "How about you? You know, it's been a while. Life isn't only about work and surf."

"Sometimes I forget," Kai said.

"You should come over one night," Jade said. "I'd be glad to help you remember."

"Remember what?" Shauna asked as she came out of the shop. She gave Kai and Jade a curious look.

"Uh, Shauna, this is Jade. Jade, Shauna," Kai said. "Jade works behind the counter at Sun Haven Surf. Shauna works behind the counter at Ice Cream."

"I guess we have something in common," Jade said.

"Looks like we might have something else in common too," Shauna said, staring at Kai.

"Well, uh, it was great to see you, Jade," Kai said. "Catch you around town, okay?"

"Sure." Jade darted forward and left a kiss on his cheek, then jogged off.

"So, ready to go to the funeral home?" Kai asked Shauna.

"Too bad it's not *her* funeral," Shauna grumbled.

They started to walk down the sidewalk. "You really have to wonder about her," Shauna said. "I mean, if I were her I'd be going out with guys my own age or older."

"Maybe she does," Kai said.

Shauna gave him a look that said she knew better. A few moments later they got to the L. Balter & Son funeral home. Kai started around the back.

"Where are you going?" Shauna asked.

"His apartment's back here," said Kai.

"He *lives* here?" Shauna asked.

"Yeah, I know," Kai said. "It's weird, but he's got a cool apartment and the rent's free."

"It better be," Shauna said.

Behind the funeral home the space where Bean's hearse was usually parked was empty. Kai rang the doorbell for Bean's apartment and waited.

"Doesn't sound like anyone's there," Shauna said.

They went back around to the front. Just as they reached the sidewalk, a tall woman wearing a black pantsuit came out and locked the front door. She had straight black hair. There was no doubt in Kai's mind that she was Bean's mother.

"Uh, excuse me?" Kai said.

The woman turned. "Yes?"

"We're friends of Bean's," Kai said. "I'm Kai and this is Shauna."

The woman smiled politely. It was clear to Kai that she had no idea who they were.

"Anyway, we usually see Bean around during the day," Kai said. "He's got Shauna's surfboard in the back of his car and—"

"Oh, you're surfing friends?" the woman said.

"Yes," said Shauna.

The woman's smile turned a little warmer. "He took the day off. I'm sure he'll be back later."

"Any idea where he went?" Kai asked, curious.

"You think he tells me? All he said was that he'd be spending the day with a friend."

"Okay, thanks," Kai said. He and Shauna started back down the sidewalk. It was time for both of them to get back to work.

"I wonder who that friend is?" Shauna said.

Kai kept his lips pressed together. The logical answer was that he was with Pauline, Shauna's cousin, on another secret get-together.

"I guess the only thing I can do is leave

another message on his cell that I'd love to get my board in the morning," Shauna said.

Kai checked his watch. "Guess I better get back to work."

They walked to the corner of Main and East Streets.

"Thanks for the ice cream," Kai said.

"Anytime," Shauna said. "At least I'm good for something in your life."

Kai understood what she meant. "Listen, Shauna, a month or so from now, I'm probably gonna leave and go somewhere far away. I mean, that's the way it's been for the past two years. You understand?"

Shauna nodded sadly. "Well, see you in the morning if Bean shows up with my board." She turned and walked away.

Kai went back to T-licious.

"Perfect timing, sonny boy," his father said when he arrived. "Sean just pulled up in back. Help him unload the new stuff. Also, later tonight or tomorrow, if you see your buddy the motel man, tell him we'll be leaving at the end of the week."

"We're moving again?" Kai asked.

"That's right, sonny boy."

Thirty-nine

The next morning the surf was up. Before dawn Kai carried his and Spazzy's boards down to the beach. He was kneeling on the sand in the dim gray predawn light when he saw Bean come down the beach carrying old #43, the long board Shauna had been using. Bean's eyes looked puffy from lack of sleep. His long black hair was pulled into a braid, but wisps of it fell out here and there and his clothes looked wrinkled.

"You okay?" Kai asked.

Bean yawned and put #43 down. "Nothing a couple of days' worth of sleep won't fix."

"Where've you been?"

"Pursuing the light at the end of the tunnel,"

Bean said, a bit mysteriously. He stretched and gazed out at the waves. "Looks good."

"Get your board."

Bean shook his head. "No way. It's bedtime for Beanzo. I just wanted to drop Shauna's board off so she could use it this morning. So, should I ask about Fairport tomorrow?"

"If I decide to do it, any chance you could give me a ride?"

"Definitely. Just leave a message on my cell." Bean started back up the beach, then stopped. "I ran into Spazzy yesterday. He asked if I could pick up his board and wet suit."

"Sure," Kai said. "How's he doing?"

"Well, you know. Jillian really freaked when she found out he's been surfing all these years."

"But that's just it," Kai said. "Doesn't it mean anything that he's been doing it all this time and he's never gotten hurt? And when he's on a board all those weird twitches go away?"

"You'd think so, wouldn't you?" Bean said. He picked up Spazzy's board and wet suit. "So listen, leave that message if you need a ride, okay?"

"Will do," Kai said. He finished waxing,

put on his leash, and headed into the water.

He paddled out in the channel along the jetty. By the time he got outside and looked back at the beach, Lucas and Buzzy were waxing up and Shauna was crossing the boardwalk. A nice set was coming in. Kai picked off a good-size wave, did a bottom turn, headed back up, did a front side snap, and angled down. The wave sectioned ahead of him so Kai went back up, catching air off the lip.

On the beach Shauna raised both hands in fists as if to cheer. Buzzy and Lucas were already in the channel along the jetty, paddling. Kai paddled back outside. It was one of those days when the larger waves were breaking in sections, but the medium-size ones were peeling more steadily. He was waiting for his next wave when Buzzy and Lucas got out there. A set came through and Lucas gave Kai a questioning look. Kai nodded back as if to say, "Go ahead, take a wave."

Lucas took off and started to slash and bash. Kai was lining up for the next wave in the set when Buzzy suddenly said, "That was a nice-looking ride before."

"Thanks," Kai replied. By now he knew better than to think Lucas's father would offer a compliment without some other motive behind it.

"A grom as good as you could figure to do pretty well at Fairport tomorrow," Lucas's father said.

Kai nodded as he paddled over to get under the peak.

"It would be good for Lucas, too," Buzzy said.

That caught Kai by surprise. He sat up on his board and let the wave roll under him. The spray from the crest rained back down on him like a momentary sun shower. "How's that?"

"He needs the competition," Buzzy said. "Someone who'll push him. You know why so many world-class surfers have come out of a small-wave break like Sebastian Inlet? They say it's the competition."

It appeared that Buzzy wanted him to compete against Lucas to make Lucas a better surfer.

"You never know," Kai said. "It might just turn out to be the other way around, with Lucas pushing me."

"All right," Buzzy said. "If that's the way it's meant to be, then that's the way it'll be. You know, I think you boys got off to a bad start.

But it doesn't have to stay that way. You and Lucas are probably the best young surfers around. You could be really good for each other."

Another set was coming in. The chat with Buzzy was interesting, but Kai wanted a wave. He turned and paddled into a medium-size curl that promised a longer, if less challenging, ride.

Kai rode it down the line, doing a small cutback here and there to stay in the curl, then hopping the board in the mush, making it almost all the way in to the part of the beach opposite Sewers, where Shauna was carrying #43 toward the water.

"Hey." He sat on his board and waited for Shauna to paddle out.

"I guess Bean got my message," Shauna said as she came out.

"I saw him this morning." Kai said, paddling beside her toward Sewers. "He dropped the board off for you."

"How come he isn't here?" Shauna asked.

"It was a little before six and it looked like he hadn't been to bed yet."

"Interesting," Shauna said.

They paddled out to Sewers and sat up on their boards, looking for waves. Down the beach, Everett, Sam, and Derek arrived.

"I guess Sam's hand has healed enough so he can surf," Kai said.

"How come you're not over at Screamers?" Shauna asked.

"I want to ask you a question," Kai said.

They sat in the waves and talked for a long time. And when they'd finished, Kai had made up his mind.

Forty

The next morning Kai sat in the shade in the Driftwood Motel parking lot with his board, towel, extra T-shirt, and a plastic bag with some bottled water and peanut-butter-and-jelly sandwiches inside. Down the street the flag in front of the bank flapped toward the south, meaning there was a nice offshore breeze to hold the wave faces open. The door to the motel office swung open and Curtis came out with two mugs of coffee, one blue and the other black.

"All fired up?" he asked, handing the black mug to Kai.

"No."

"Good. Save that stoke for when you need it."

Kai shrugged and took a sip of the coffee. He winced at the taste of the whisky. That stuff was strong. He handed the mug back to Curtis. "Think you got your mugs mixed up."

"Sorry." Curtis gave him the blue one. "I do like a little whisky with my coffee."

"Tasted more like you like a little coffee with your whisky," Kai said.

Curtis smiled and raised his mug. "Top o' the morning to ya."

Kai took a sip from the blue mug. That was better.

"So you're off to do battle against the son of the dark warlord of evil, huh?"

"I guess."

"Don't act so excited, grom. Your eagerness is overwhelming."

"I guess part of me still thinks the whole thing is stupid, that's all."

"It ain't too late to back out."

Kai shrugged. He'd made up his mind.

"I also hear you're movin' out tonight," Curtis said.

"Yeah," Kai said. "My father found a basement for us to stay in for the next month."

"You don't have to go, grom," Curtis said.

"You can stay here if you want. At least till the Feds get the place."

"'Feds'?" Kai repeated uncertainly.

"Back taxes," Curtis explained. "Appears I've been a bit negligent in my bookkeeping. Looks like if Buzzy don't get me, the tax man might."

"Is it serious?" Kai asked.

"Don't know yet, grom."

Bean pulled up in the hearse.

"Now there's an optimistic mode of transportation given your intended purpose," Curtis said with a smile.

Kai picked up his stuff. "Catch you later, old man."

"Who knows? If there's nothing good on TV, I might even come over and watch," said Curtis.

Kai put his stuff in the back of the hearse and got in front with Bean, who pulled back onto Seaside Drive. Jazz was playing on the sound system.

"Who's this?" Kai asked.

"Wes Montgomery, king of the jazz guitar."

"It's good."

"You expected bad?" Bean said. "Hey, I have to admit I was surprised when you called.

What made you change your mind and decide to enter?"

"Guess it's just gotten to the point where it's easier to do it than to keep explaining why I don't want to."

"Psyched?" Bean asked.

"Not particularly," Kai said. "You?"

"A little. But what do I have to lose?" Bean asked. "Long board competitions are like women's golf. No one except the participants really cares."

They rode along Seaside Drive listening to the jazz. A Jeep passed in the opposite direction.

"That reminds me," Bean said. "You do anything about Goldilocks yet?"

"Not yet."

"Dude, the longer you wait, the more chance there is he's gonna unload those boards," Bean said. "And once they're gone, you've got no evidence against him."

"I know."

The Fairport town parking lot was jammed with people pulling boards off car racks and out of the backs of pickups. There were families with gremmies and groms, and old guys with long boards there to compete in the legends division. A lot of the families brought chairs and umbrellas and coolers. It was going to be an all-day competition.

Kai and Bean grabbed their stuff and headed for the beach, which was crowded with parents putting up umbrellas and opening chairs while contestants stretched and waxed their boards. Serious amateur photographers were setting up tripods, and a crowd of walk-in entrants hovered in front of a big white open-faced tent, filling out last-minute entry forms. Trucks from Quiksilver and Billabong were there, and a big banner over the tent read FAIRPORT SURF. Packs of girls and guys roamed around talking to their friends and gabbing on cell phones. Kai and Bean put down their stuff and walked over to the tent. Inside was a long table manned by some women writing down entrants' names. Behind them were some smaller tables where walkie-talkies sat charging off a car battery. A handful of men and women—no doubt the contest organizers and judges—stood around talking.

"Well, well, look who's here," a voice behind them said.

Kai and Bean turned around. It was Jade.

"Hey," Kai said. "Women's long board or short board?"

"Can't I go both ways?" Jade asked. "Double your pleasure, double your fun. How about you?"

"I'm short." Kai jerked his head at Bean. "He's long."

"Really?" Jade gave Bean an interested look. "How long?"

"Uh, a little over nine feet," Bean said. He nodded toward the water. "Good day, huh?"

"Pretty good right now," Jade said.

"What are they predicting?" Kai asked.

"Waist to shoulder high with some larger sets," Jade said. "The big unknown is going to be the wind. If it turns onshore like it usually does, it's gonna be a mess by this afternoon."

"What kind of break is it?" Kai asked.

"Sandbar," Jade said. "So it's kind of shifty depending on the tide and wind. One minute it's breaking in one spot. Five minutes later it's breaking fifty yards down the beach. You really have to watch it and pick your spots."

They signed in and were told to wait for their event to be called over the loudspeaker.

Kai and Bean said they'd see Jade later and went back to their stuff.

"Hey, guys!" Spazzy was jogging along the beach toward them with his board under his arm. Behind him came Shauna with Jillian.

"Am I seeing things?" Kai asked Bean.

"Oh, guess I forgot to tell you," Bean said with a grin.

Jillian came through the crowd looking around with an expression like she was walking through the monkey cage at the zoo. She was pulling some kind of bright blue plastic thing that reminded Kai of a NASA space vehicle designed for exploring the surfaces of other planets. It had big wheels for rolling across the sand, with a built-in umbrella, cooler, and basket for towels. When all that stuff was removed, it could be turned upside down to become a beach chair.

When Spazzy's sister saw Bean, a big smile appeared on her face. Kai watched in disbelief as she actually walked up and kissed him on the cheek. "Hi!"

"This is so cool!" Spazzy was twitching and ticking so much that Kai wondered if he'd exhaust himself.

"You're gonna compete?" Kai asked.

"What do you think, dude?" Spazzy asked. He pointed at the white tent. "Is that the sign-in?"

"You bet."

"Gotta go sign in." Spazzy headed for the tent.

Jillian was instantly alert to her brother moving toward a group of strangers who might not understand his behavior. "I'll do it for you."

"No," Spazzy said. "I'll do it. It's my competition." He got on the line, twitching and ticking and making funny sounds. Some gremmies in front of him turned and stared, then whispered to each other and made faces.

Spazzy hardly seemed to care. Then again, he had to be so used to it that it didn't matter. Jillian started to unpack the space vehicle. For the moment, Kai, Shauna, and Bean were alone.

"How?" Kai asked in a low voice.

"You know all that sleep Bean said he *wasn't* getting?" Shauna said.

Bean blushed and scuffed his foot on the sand.

"You did it just for Spazzy?" Kai asked.

"No way!" Bean blurted out. "Dude, this is

for real. She is beautiful and brilliant. I mean, sure, I argued on Spazzy's behalf, but either way, I'm totally jazzed."

Kai couldn't believe it. Just the idea of Jillian in the passenger seat of Bean's hearse was a hard one to swallow. The rest was simply amazing.

Spazzy came back. "This is so cool! I've never been to a competition before. And I'm *in* this one."

"I had no idea so many people surfed," Jillian said, gazing around at the crowd.

"My guess is there are about a hundred and fifty surfers here," Bean said. "The rest are families and friends."

"And in some cases," Shauna added, looking past them, "enemies."

Kai followed her eyes. Lucas and his crew were coming toward them.

Forty-one

"**W**ell, if it ain't Mr. Competition himself," Sam said with a smirk.

Kai ignored the taunt and looked around. Runt was there, but Everett and Derek weren't. "Where's Everett?" he asked.

"Said he had something else to do," Lucas said.

That seemed a little strange to Kai. Next to Lucas, Everett was probably the best surfer in the crew.

"Well, see you out there," Kai said.

Lucas nodded. He and his brahs headed over to the tent to sign in.

Kai and his friends commenced to do what competitive surfers everywhere spent most of their time doing at competitions—waiting and watching. The first rounds of the day would be fifteen-minute heats. Six surfers would compete in each heat, with three eliminated and three moving on to the next round. The men went first, then the boys. Next came the juniors—the group Kai, Spazzy, and Lucas's crew were in. Everyone listened for the first heat to be called: "Rodney, Jackson, Herter, Moncure, Rhodes, and Winthrop."

"We're in the same heat!" Spazzy said to Kai, then jumped up and grabbed his board.

Kai picked up his board.

"Good luck!" Jillian called. "Be careful!"

Spazzy and Kai walked over to the pole where the event flags were. The beach marshal was handing out colored jerseys. Spazzy got a light blue one and Kai got yellow. Soon all six contestants were gathered around the marshal. They eyed one another, trying to figure out who the serious contenders were. Spazzy twitched and made some strange noises.

"Okay, boys, we want you to have fun out there," the marshal said. "Just keep it clean and respect one another's spaces. No snaking or drop-ins. We're pretty serious about that. Any interference will result in automatic disqualification." He checked his watch. "We're doing water starts today, so you can head out there now. Soon as the green flag goes up, you can start to surf. It's a fifteen-minute heat. We'll give you an air horn and yellow flag when there are five minutes left."

The six contestants hit the water. Two of the kids, one in pink and the other in white, started to paddle hard, as if they were in a race. Spazzy started after them, afraid they might get a head start.

"Hey," Kai called in a low voice, trying not to attract the other surfers.

Spazzy turned back. "Yeah?"

"Don't waste your strength," Kai said. "It's a water start. They won't raise the green flag until we're all out there. Those guys are just burning adrenaline."

Spazzy slowed down. "Thanks."

The six surfers got outside. The air horn blew and the green flag went up. Almost immediately, pink and white tried to get rides on waves that were going nowhere. Kai had a feeling that unless one of them got incredibly lucky, those two weren't going to be much to worry about.

A set came in, and navy blue caught a wave and did a snap with a nice spray, then tried to get into the pocket again but ran out of juice. Kai knew he'd be a contender. The next wave in the set was rearing up, and both Spazzy and Kai were close enough to take it.

"Go on," Kai said.

Spazzy paddled into the wave and popped up. The wave looked like it might peel without sectioning, and rather than try a ride-ending trick, Spazzy wisely decided to go for distance and length of ride. Kai heard hoots and cheers from the beach.

Another wave was coming and Kai and the remaining surfer, a kid wearing red, paddled for it. Kai was farther inside so it was his ride, but the other guy either didn't see him or thought maybe he could steal the wave. With the kid blocking him and no room to go anywhere, Kai did a sharp bottom turn, went up vertical behind the other surfer and tried to get some air going over the lip. In no time his ride was over and he bailed. When his head came back out of the water, he could hear a voice distorted by a megaphone. He couldn't make out the words, but he knew the meaning: The guy in red had just been disqualified.

Since his ride had been cut short, Kai didn't have far to paddle to get outside again. By now Spazzy had come back from his long ride.

"Too bad that guy dropped in on you," Spazzy said. "Looked like a nice wave."

"That's life," Kai said. "Looked like you had a good ride."

"Good? You mean great," Spazzy said. "I really lucked out."

Another set was coming in. "See if you can do it again," Kai said.

"You sure?" Spazzy asked. "I already got one."

"So get another," Kai said.

Spazzy took off on the first good wave. This one looked like it might close out ahead of him, so he threw some spray with a snap, then tried to scoot around in front of the breaking section in the hope of getting past it. The white water caught him and he bailed out.

The other guys caught some waves, but didn't do much with them. Then Kai took off on one and actually managed to get a half-decent cutback and tailslide out of it. Once again he heard hoots and cheers from the crowd on the beach.

The air horn went off again. The green flag went down and the yellow went up. As if desperate for a last chance to prove themselves, pink and white grabbed the first waves that came along and again couldn't do much with them. Spazzy caught another and smartly went for distance and duration again. Kai kept glancing at his watch, then at navy blue, and then the incoming waves. He and navy blue could almost read each other's minds. Given the choice, they both wanted the last ride. It was like a game of dare. Who'd go first? But with only five surfers in the heat and three going for sure to the next round, Kai was already pretty certain Spazzy had made it and he had nothing to lose.

A wave came. At the last second Kai spun around. It wasn't that he was trying to fake out navy blue, but he wanted to take the wave late and the face steep, to get up enough speed to boost air. With the sound of the folding lip crackling in his ears, he took off and popped up, compressed into the bottom turn and launched off the lip, rotating as hard as he could, without a clue as to how he was going to land.

It felt sort of between a one-eighty and a

flip, and the amazing thing was, he actually landed on his board before pitching headfirst into the wash. When his head popped out, it was just in time to hear the final air horn and see the yellow flag come down and the red one come up.

The first heat was over.

Forty-two

Kai started to paddle in. The six entrants in the next heat were already on their way out. Lucas and Sam had been thrown together with four other surfers Kai had never seen before. As Kai passed Lucas, he said, "Good luck." Lucas scowled back. To Kai it was an insight into how the guy's brain worked. Everything was either black or white, friend or enemy, good or bad. There was nothing in between.

Kai got to the beach, returned his jersey, and headed for his friends. The judges were still tabulating the results of his heat and had not yet announced which of the contestants would move on to the next round. Jillian,

Shauna, and Bean were all on their feet, waiting for him.

"What was that last move?" Bean asked. "I'm not sure I've ever seen anything like it."

"That's probably because it's completely unmakeable," Kai said.

"It was still awesome," said Shauna.

"Thanks." Kai turned to Spazzy. "Smart wave selection. Smart rides."

"Thanks," Spazzy said. "I figured I'd rather be safe than sorry. Besides, I really wanted to get past this round since I'll definitely get killed in the next one."

"Why do you say that?" Jillian asked.

"I don't have the moves or tricks," Spazzy said.

"Hey, you never know," Bean said. "One good wave is all you need."

The air horn sounded and the green flag went up for the next heat. Kai and the others watched the six surfers in Lucas's group start to ride. Sam caught a wave and did his signature snap, throwing huge spray. Kai had a feeling Lucas had shared the surf-wax-on-the-fins trick with him.

Meanwhile, on the beach, the beach marshal with the megaphone cleared his throat.

"Your attention please," he announced. "The contestants from the last heat who will move to the next round are Herter, Rodney, and Winthrop."

"We made it!" Spazzy cried.

Everyone exchanged high fives. Spazzy was so excited, and twitching so hard, he missed most of them, so the others patted him on the back.

"Now what happens?" Jillian asked.

"We wait," Bean said. "It'll be a while until the next round."

The sun was overhead by now, cooking everyone on the beach. The heat, plus the salt from the water, made Kai and the others thirsty. Kai took out a bottle of water and finished it. Jillian had water for herself and Spazzy. A little while later the men's long board heat was announced and Bean got up and stretched. Everyone wished him good luck as he picked up his board and went to get a jersey.

"I can see the difference between a long board and a short board," Jillian said after he'd left. "Why would he choose one and not the other?"

"The long board's more traditional," Kai

answered. "It's easier to ride, but harder to look good. To me it's real subtle. More of the thinking man's board. Kind of an intellectual thing."

"Really?" Jillian seemed to like hearing that.

They watched Bean paddle out wearing a white jersey. There were only five competitors in his heat. Kai wasn't surprised. Long board competitors were definitely in the minority. The five long boarders got outside. The air horn went off and the green flag went up.

For the next ten minutes they watched the long boarders ride mostly for distance and duration. Here and there someone would try an off-the-lip, but it mostly just looked like any old day at the beach.

"It certainly is different," Jillian observed with a yawn.

The air horn sounded and the yellow flag went up. By now hardly anyone on the beach was even watching. It was Shauna who got their attention.

"Guys," she said.

Everyone turned and looked. Bean was in the pocket of a wave, crouched down, five toes over the nose, arms stretched out in front of him. Classic cheater five position. A few hoots and cheers rose up from the crowd, and more heads began to turn. As the wave gave out, Bean cross-stepped back to the tail and turned the board around just in time to catch the re-formed inside break. It was closing out, and he turned the board once again, this time heading straight in. Then he grabbed the rails, bent over and placed his head on the deck, and did a headstand, his long black braid actually hanging off the side of the board and dragging in the water.

By now the whole beach was watching, hooting and cheering.

"Is . . . is that allowed?" Jillian stammered.

"Only if you're Bean," Shauna said.

After that ride Bean didn't even bother to go back out and finish the heat. He didn't have to. Back on the beach everyone congratulated him, then settled down and waited for the next set of junior heats to begin.

Nearly two hours passed before the call came. Again it was a three out of six elimination. The names were called off. Spazzy was grouped with Sam and four other surfers.

"Oh, well, it was fun while it lasted." Spazzy shrugged.

"That's the spirit." Bean slapped him on the back. "Quit while you're ahead."

"I wouldn't even bother going out there," Kai said. "Why not just give up now? It's a lot better than facing all that humiliation."

"We could just pack up and leave, and they wouldn't even notice you were gone," Shauna said.

Spazzy grinned. "You guys suck." He picked up his board and headed for the tent to get his jersey.

"Does he really not stand a chance?" Jillian asked after he'd left.

"Hard to say," Bean said.

"You never know," added Kai.

Forty-three

This batch of surfers was a lot better than the last. Most went for slash-and-gash tricks. Once again Spazzy bucked the trend and went for number and length of rides. When the heat was over, Bean and Kai traded looks and shook their heads. There was no way to tell whether Jillian's brother had made it or not.

Spazzy stripped off his jersey and ran back to Kai and his friends. Seawater dripped out of his hair, and he was breathing hard and had the biggest smile on his face.

"What'd you think?" he asked. For that moment he didn't twitch at all. It was as if he'd forgotten. Kai watched Jillian's face as she saw the effect surfing had on her brother's condition.

"I think that no matter what, you're great," his sister said.

Of course, Spazzy immediately started twitching like an electric wire, but somehow that was okay.

The beach marshal announced the results of Spazzy's heat. "Moncure, Sarnoff, and Winthrop."

"I made it!" Spazzy's shout of joy was so loud that people all around looked up and smiled. He threw his arms around Kai's neck and hugged him.

"I guess that's the definition of stoked," Bean quipped.

Once again Kai stole a peek at Jillian. He wasn't sure who looked happier, Spazzy or his sister.

A little while later Bean went out for the finals of the long board competition.

"Why are there only three surfers?" Jillian asked.

"With only five contestants, they only needed two heats," Kai explained. "So who-ever wins this is the winner."

Jillian clasped her hands together. "You mean, Larry could win the whole thing?"

Kai still couldn't get used to anyone call-ing Bean by his real name. "Right," Kai said.

"He could win the whole thing right now."

Jillian let out a small gasp. Kai winked at Shauna.

The air horn blew and the green flag went up. The three long boarders took turns catching waves. Bean got another nice cheater five on one ride. One of the other long boarders had more or less the same move. As the heat wound down, Kai could not have predicted who the winner would be. Both Shauna and Jillian seemed to have grown tired of watching heat after heat and were talking.

The five-minute air horn went off and the yellow flag went up. Out in the water Bean spotted a wave and turned his board toward shore. With an effortless, almost lazy-looking stroke he caught it, stood up, and angled along the face.

With his knees slightly bent and his arms hanging loosely at his sides, Bean stood motionless, as if content to ride the wave out. Only then did Kai realize that his friend was gradually getting ahead of the bowl. Suddenly Bean swung his arms and upper torso around in a huge, sweeping roundhouse cutback.

Kai had never seen Bean pull a move like it before. It seemed as if no one on the beach even noticed. Kai glanced at the judges. All three were busy scribbling on their clipboards. Kai felt a smile grow on his face. At least the people who kept score had noticed.

Way to go, Bean.

Winners wouldn't be announced until the awards ceremony at the end of the day, but Kai had no doubt who the men's long board champ would be.

The final air horn blew, and a few minutes later Bean walked up the beach with his board tucked under his arm. Jillian looked up from her conversation with Shauna. "How'd you do?" she asked.

"Okay," Bean said, picking up a towel and drying his face.

"That last move was pretty nice," Kai said.

"Thanks," Bean said. "It felt good."

The beach was emptier now. The sun had moved well past the midpoint of the day and many of the eliminated competitors had packed up and left. The mood among those who remained had changed. The lighthearted, what-the-hell feeling had been replaced with something grimmer and more serious. Kai was thirsty. He'd finished all his water and was angry at himself for not bringing more. He was tempted to ask Jillian for some, but she was getting pretty low too.

"Know what's amazing?" Shauna said. "More than half the crowd's gone, but everyone in our group is still in the competition."

The same, Kai noted to himself, was true of Lucas's crew. Sam and Lucas were still in the juniors, and Runt had made it to the semifinals of the boys' division. Buzzy had also arrived. Apparently he'd been confident his son would make it through the earlier heats and hadn't bothered to watch. But now he was not only there, he had taken Lucas away from his friends, as if he felt his son needed to be less distracted and more focused on the competition. Lucas dutifully listened and nodded as his father spoke and pointed at the waves.

A guy carrying a clipboard and a large plastic bag strolled up to the blanket where Kai and his friends were sitting. He had black hair and was wearing khaki shorts and a green polo shirt that said "Bonzo Kreem" on it.

"Hey, dudes, talk to you for a second?" he said.

Kai and the others nodded.

"I'm Mark Curlin from Bonzo Kreem," he said. "You ever hear of our product?"

Kai and the others shook their heads. Curlin reached into the plastic bag and took out a bunch of sample-size orange-and-green plastic tubes and tossed them around. "Bonzo Kreem is new on the market. A kind of all-in-one salve for your typical surf-related skin disorders. It works on chafing, wax rash, jock itch, fungus, and sunburn. It's waterproof and hypoallergenic, and if you leave it on for a couple of days, it produces a pheromone that drives the ladies wild." Curlin grinned. "Naw, just kidding about the last part, but everything else I said is true and laboratory tested. So I hope you guys'll try these samples and keep us in mind. We're putting together the Bonzo Kreem Dream Team and we'll be watching the results of today's competition. Peace out, dudes."

Curlin moved on to the next group of surfers.

"Do you realize what he just said?" Bean asked. "We could be on the Bonzo Kreem Dream Team, spreading waterproof jock itch cream to the far corners of the Earth."

"Gee whiz, Mr. Bean, are you really a professionally sponsored surfer?" Shauna pretended to be surf groupie.

"You betcha," Bean answered in a deep baritone. "Got a problem with chafing, young lady?"

"Well, not really, Mr. Bean," Shauna answered.

"How about wax rash?"

Shauna shook her head.

"Jock itch?"

"I beg your pardon, Mr. Bean." Shauna pretended to be insulted.

"Well, then, perhaps it's sunburn we need to talk about."

By now Shauna was pretending to look elsewhere. "Oh, look, there's the guys on the Deep Pit Surf Deodorant Team. See you later, Mr. Bonzo Kreem Bean."

"But wait!" Bean pretended to call desperately. "We haven't talked about fungus!"

They were interrupted by the beach marshal on the megaphone. "For the semifinals of the juniors we'll have two four-man, twenty-minute heats. Two from each heat will go on to the finals. First semifinal heat will be Winthrop, Keller, Frank, and Herter."

"That's us!" Spazzy jumped to his feet and grabbed his board. "Come on, Kai."

By now the competitors didn't have to be

briefed on what to do. They went to the tent to get their jerseys. Kai and Lucas arrived at the table at the same time.

"Not bad for a guy who says he hates to compete," Lucas said as he accepted the black jersey.

"You talking about me or you?" Kai asked as he took the white jersey.

Lucas frowned.

A moment later they were paddling out. Spazzy had gotten the green jersey and the kid named Keller had the red. The second Lucas got outside, he turned his board around, caught a decent, but not great, wave, and ripped. It appeared to Kai that Buzzy had given his son a new strategy—put pressure on the other surfers. Get out ahead as soon as possible and make the others nervous. Force them to play catch-up. Kai understood the strategy. A nervous, anxious surfer was more likely to pick a bad wave, or try something too difficult on a good one.

The logical response was to take your time and wait.

A decent set came in and both Spazzy and the guy named Keller took off on the same wave. Spazzy was farther inside and up first, but had to bail when Keller popped in front of him. Kai doubted Keller dropped in on him on purpose. More likely the guy was feeling the pressure from Lucas, saw a good wave, and went for it without looking. But it didn't matter. A whistle blew and the beach marshal called red in. Keller had been disqualified.

That left Lucas, Kai, and Spazzy. Lucas got another short, but half-decent ride. Of the three surfers now left in the heat, he was the only one who'd even scored a point. While Lucas paddled out, Spazzy and Kai waited for the next good wave. A set came in, and Kai saw instantly that it was out of Spazzy's reach. It was Kai's wave if he wanted it. He turned and paddled.

The wave jacked up under him and Kai felt as if he'd stepped into an elevator and been boosted up a floor higher than he'd expected. He suddenly found himself on the lip of the thing, looking straight down the face into a deep blue trough. It was like sitting on top of a high wall. Had he sat back on his board, the wave would have rolled right under him.

But Kai had no intention of sitting back. Only a few times in his life had he popped up on his board and found himself airborne on the way down. The board hit water and Kai did a sharp bottom turn and headed back up, easily getting vertical and doing an off-the-lip before it even felt like the ride had begun. What happened from that point on was strictly unconscious. Kai would later swear it felt as if the board simply did whatever it wanted to. Cutback, method, floater . . . It almost felt like the wave was having too much fun with him to want to stop.

Kai could hear the cheers and hoots before the ride even ended. There'd definitely been luck involved. Somehow he'd found himself on a wave that didn't want to quit. But he'd also taken advantage of what it had to offer.

When he paddled back out, Kai wasn't surprised to see the glum expression on Lucas's face. The guy knew he'd been completely outsurfed. What did surprise Kai was when Lucas nodded and grudgingly said, "Nice ride."

Kai paddled up over the next wave. There was Spazzy, sitting on his board, shoulders hunched, looking even more bummed than Lucas.

Only then did Kai realize what he'd done.

Forty-four

"**G**reat ride," Spazzy said.

Kai could tell he meant it, but that he was also devastated. Kai thought he knew what had happened. Spazzy had come to Fairport that day without expectations. He only had those crazy fantasies all kids had about miracle rides and being declared the champ. The kind of fantasies you know never come true, but you cling to anyway. Then Spazzy made it through the first two rounds and found himself in the semifinals. A place he'd never expected to be. Just one round from the finals and the possible championship. Suddenly the impossible seemed possible. After all, in any given heat anything could happen. Your opponent could break his board. You could find yourself on the wave of the day. Who knew?

And so somehow, between the last round and this round, Spazzy had begun to think that maybe winning the event wasn't a total fantasy. That it was within his grasp. And the truth was, at the beginning of the semifinal heat, that had been the case. Spazzy, Lucas, Keller, and Kai had paddled as equals. But things had quickly changed. Keller was disqualified, Lucas had turned in two solid rides, and Kai had just come off a monster rip. As a result, Spazzy's fantasies, hopes, and dreams were crashing down like the waves they were supposed to be riding.

A mediocre wave came in. Five minutes ago, no one would have taken it. But feeling the pressure, Spazzy took off on it.

"So now what do you do?"

Kai turned and found Lucas paddling close to him.

"Right now you and I are a lock for the next round," Lucas said, as if Kai didn't already know. "Of course, that means your buddy's finished."

"There's still time," Kai replied.

Lucas gave him a "Yeah, right" look, but said nothing more.

A lull in the waves followed. Nothing worth riding was coming in or even visible on the horizon. Lucas and Kai sat on their boards waiting and watching. It wasn't long before Spazzy joined them.

No one said a word. No one had to.

The air horn blared. The green flag went down and the yellow went up. Five minutes to go and Spazzy hadn't had anything that even approached a decent ride. Kai spied the peak of a wave out beyond the others. A new set was coming in.

"Hey, Lucas," he said. "Why not let Spazzy get one of these. It won't make any difference to your score. You've already got enough points to move on to the finals."

Lucas tilted his head as if considering it. "Maybe I do. But you don't."

"Maybe I don't care," Kai answered.

"Forget it, guys," Spazzy said. "I don't want any handouts."

"It's not a handout," Kai said. "It's just a chance to show what you've got. Besides, if Lucas and I agree, what difference does it make?"

Lucas gazed out at the approaching set. "Suppose we do it this way: I get the first good one, and then you can give Spazzy the next?"

"As long as you agree to take the first or second wave in the set," Kai said.

"Deal," said Lucas.

The set came in and, as agreed, Lucas took off first.

Kai turned to Spazzy. "Get the next one, dude. It's all yours."

"Thanks, Kai." Spazzy paddled into the next wave. From Kai's viewpoint behind, everything looked good. He expected to see Spazzy's head and shoulders pop up. It didn't happen. A second later Spazzy's board pinwheeled into the air. The leash went tight and the board hurtled back down.

Kai checked his watch. Three minutes left.

Spazzy had missed what was probably his last shot.

With two minutes left, Lucas paddled back out.

"Looks like your plan didn't work," he said.

Kai watched Spazzy paddle toward them through the waves, trying to get out in time for one last ride. The kid had a desperate, fearful look on his face—as if he just didn't want it to end like this. Kai looked back out to see if anything decent was coming in. There were some dark wave crests out there rising above the others, but nothing particularly big or impressive. Probably nothing that would give Spazzy the kind of platform he needed to get a really stellar ride.

"Hey, look at it this way," Lucas said. "Your friend had a good run."

He had, and Kai was glad for him. This meant something to Spazzy. It wasn't just about competing. It was about showing people what a kid with a disability could do. But what did it mean to Kai? Why should he care whether he got to the finals or not? Wasn't this what he hated about surfing? The competition. Here for a trophy. There for a sponsorship, and in most places, just for another wave. If this competition didn't mean anything to him, but meant so much to Spazzy, what was Kai doing out there?

The next set was coming. The one neither Kai nor Lucas needed to get into the finals. The one that simply didn't have enough juice to help Spazzy get a decent ride.

"Might as well get a few extra points for the ride in," Lucas said, and started to paddle.

Suddenly Kai had an idea.

Forty-five

Kai proned out on his board and started to paddle as hard as he could. There was no way he was going to catch the wave, but that wasn't what he was trying to do. Just a few feet from him, Lucas was also paddling. But those few feet were the difference between catching it and not catching it. Kai was counting on Lucas to turn and look back at the wave. And when he did, he was in for a surprise.

Lucas looked back over his shoulder. When he saw Kai just behind and to his right, his eyes widened. He had to know that if they both kept going, there was a good chance Kai would hit him.

Lucas pulled up into a stall and let the wave

pass. Kai kept going and caught it, then purposefully allowed himself to bite it in the trough. When his head came up out of the soup, he could hear the shrilled tremolo of the air horn. He'd just managed to get himself disqualified.

Lucas was paddling toward him with an angry look on his face. "What the fuck was that?" he yelled.

Kai just smiled and held on to his board. "I don't know what I was thinking, Lucas. Guess I won't be seeing you in the finals after all."

He started to paddle in.

"Hey!" Spazzy called from behind, and paddled to catch up to Kai. "What happened out there?"

"I never saw him," Kai lied as they paddled in side by side. "I was so focused on catching that wave."

"But you didn't even need it," Spazzy said.

"You never know," Kai said. "You can't tell what the judges are thinking."

"But now you're out of the contest," Spazzy said.

"I know." Kai tried to look grim. "Guess you'll have to do it for me."

The first person to greet Kai on the beach

was Buzzy Frank with a major glower on his face. "What the hell was that?"

"I didn't see him," Kai said as Lucas joined them.

"The hell you didn't."

"Look," Kai said. "What do you care? Lucas won that heat hands down. He's in the finals. That's the only thing that matters, right?"

Buzzy frowned at him, then turned to his son. "Come on, let's go."

Buzzy marched away, but Lucas didn't follow. Instead he studied Kai. "You had the best single-wave score of the day. You were a lock for the finals. You knew I was on that wave. You interfered on purpose. Why?"

"Something came up," Kai said. "Something more important than winning."

Lucas scowled at him like he couldn't understand.

"Come on, Lucas," Buzzy called.

Lucas left to join his father, and Kai walked up the beach with his board tucked under his arm. Spazzy had already gone ahead to his sister, Shauna, and Bean.

"I'm in the finals!" he cried. "Can you believe it?"

"Way to go." Bean patted him on the shoulder.

"I mean, come on, Jillian," Spazzy said to his sister. "If I'm good enough to make it to the finals, I must be good enough to go surfing by myself back in Sun Haven, right?"

Jillian pursed her lips and frowned. "As long as you're with a friend."

"Promise you won't change your mind?" Spazzy asked.

"Promise," his sister said.

Spazzy grinned. "This has to be the best day of my life." He seemed to have trouble swallowing. "Man, I am thirsty. Do we have any water?"

"We ran out," Jillian said.

"I'll go get some," Spazzy said.

Ever protective of her little brother, Jillian got up. "I'll go with you."

They headed up the beach to the snack bar. As soon as they were out of earshot, Bean turned to Kai. "Interesting move out there. Tough break, getting disqualified on a garbage wave you had no reason to take. Especially considering you had the highest single-wave score of the day."

"Yeah."

"Real stroke of luck for Spazzy," Bean said. "Imagine. It's the kid's first competition ever and he's made it to the finals. Too bad he'll totally get pounded by Lucas."

"He said this is the best day of his life," said Shauna.

"Funny how that worked out, isn't it?" Bean asked.

"Life is strange," Kai said.

The three of them smiled.

Look for the next Impact Zone book!
Close Out
by Todd Strasser

The tense mist of competition was thick in the air. This wasn't some small, local, "let's all go out and have fun" kind of event. No one smiled or joked. When Kai looked around, he saw nothing but grim determination on the faces of his fellow competitors. And there were plenty of good surfers out there. People who could rip and work a wave until there was nothing left but soup. Kai surfed with total resolve, concentration, and intensity. Tomorrow he could go back to being a soul surfer.

It was a long day, and by midafternoon everyone from Sun Haven except Kai, Lucas, and Bean had been eliminated. Bean was in the men's long board finals when Booger, Spazzy, and Jillian showed up.

"Hey, guys!" Spazzy twitched as he wound his way through the patchwork of blankets, beach towels, and umbrellas. Booger and Jillian followed. Kai could see from the way Jillian kept swiveling her head that she was looking for Bean.

"He's out there." Kai pointed out at the break, where six long boarders in colored jerseys were jockeying for waves.

"How's he doing?" Booger asked.

"Hard to tell," Kai said. "They're all good. At this point it probably has as much to do with luck as anything else."

An air horn blared twice. Bean's heat was over. A few minutes later he trudged up the beach with his board under his arm and seawater dripping off the end of his long braided ponytail. His head was down and it was hard to tell whether he was bummed or just tired. But when he saw Jillian, he straightened up and smiled.

"How come you're not over at the tent waiting for the results?" Booger asked.

"They don't announce the winners until the awards ceremony," Bean said, sounding dejected. "But I didn't get enough good rides. It's unbelievable out there. You can hardly get on a wave. Every time you think you're ready to go, there's some other dude already paddling into it."

"You mean they're snaking you?" Booger asked.

"Maybe, but it's hard to tell," Bean said.

"These guys just know where to be. No matter how deep in the pocket you think you are, there's always someone a little deeper."

Jillian put her hand on Bean's shoulder.

"This the way you remember it?" Kai asked Curtis.

The older man shook his head. "The competition's fiercer, the stakes are bigger. These guys are in top shape. Look at 'em. Their shoulders, and arms, and legs. You can see they train like athletes. Back in my day, we competed hard, but there was a feeling that you still let everyone have his shot. That's not here anymore. You don't get your shot unless you fight for it. That fight starts in a gym, lifting weights, and on a track, doing endurance work. When I was on the circuit, the only things we lifted were boards and beer bottles. There are boys out there today doing things world champions weren't doing when I competed."

"Well, sure," Bean teased. "Back in those days it wasn't easy to catch air on a hundred-and-eighty-pound, fifteen-foot solid redwood board."

"Screw you," Curtis growled in a good-natured way. "By the end of my time on the tour they were starting to use short boards. The forerunners of what you kids are on today."

"Men's open finals," the beach marshal announced through the megaphone. "Competitors get your jerseys."

Kai rose to his feet and picked up his board. His friends wished him good luck.

"You can do it, Kai."

"Give it your best shot, dude."

Todd Strasser is the author of more than one hundred novels for teens and middle graders including the best-selling Help! I'm Trapped In . . . series. His novels for older teens include *The Accident, The Wave, Give a Boy a Gun,* and *Can't Get There from Here.* Todd and his kids have surfed Hawaii, California, and the eastern seaboard from Florida to New York.

Check Your **PULSE** Book Club

Sign up for the CHECK YOUR PULSE
free teen e-mail book club!

 ★ **FEATURING** ★

A new book discussion every month

Monthly book giveaways

Chapter excerpts

Book discussions with the authors

Literary horoscopes

Plus YOUR comments!

To sign up go to www.simonsays.com/simonpulse and
don't forget to CHECK YOUR PULSE!

As many as 1 in 3 Americans
who have HIV...don't know it.

**TAKE CONTROL.
KNOW YOUR STATUS.
GET TESTED.**

To learn more about HIV testing,
or get a free guide to HIV and
other sexually transmitted diseases:

**www.knowhivaids.org
1-866-344-KNOW**